ZINGARESE

A Story of Love and Life

M. Carolina Bento

To the ones who live by the truth

CONTENTS

CHAPTER ONE

DANCING

I have been living in Washington, DC for the past year, and I had a strenuously busy and demanding time during the 2012 campaign and election.

In January my friend Deborah invited me to one of the presidential inaugural balls. I met Deborah, an anchor for a major media network, years ago when I came for an internship on Capitol Hill, where I completed training as a website producer and reporter for my master's in journalism. As an established Washington, DC reporter at that time, she was a mentor, welcoming and supportive of the younger journalists.

"Life is not only about work, Lissa, you need a little fun too. Randall got tickets for the Armed Services Ball, come with us!"

Randall is Deborah's longtime boyfriend, he has a youthful spirit, always upbeat, he is delightful company! He was in the military before, now he works at the State Department.

I met him when I transferred to DC last year and Deborah generously offered me her beautiful apartment in Kalorama until I got my own place close to Dupont Circle, not far from hers. During that time I could observe what a warm and supportive relationship they have, I never had anything like that in my life. As a matter of fact I have avoided close relationships, I have my reasons...

"Thank you, Deborah, I know that the balls are a must-go fixture of Washington's social calendar after the Presidential

Inauguration, but I don't have anything to wear. To tell you the truth I never owned a ball gown."

"Let's go to Wisconsin Avenue! I'm sure you will find a fabulous dress in one of those fine stores and I'm going to get something new for myself, too."

I went along, Deborah's cheerfulness motivated me. We got dresses, had a fun winter afternoon even under the cold and slushy weather. We made it!

The next evening she and Randall stopped by to drive me to the ball at the National Building Museum. I was excited with anticipation, I have been somewhat of a recluse, avoiding social gatherings, but I'm stepping out this time. My first opportunity to attend a presidential inaugural ball is something that shouldn't be missed!

In the crowded and noisy ballroom we met some people that I have become familiar with during the course of this past year in DC, but I stayed alone at the side, feeling a little awkward, observing the enthusiastic crowd while Deborah and Randall went to the dance floor.

After they came back Randall spotted a friend across the dance floor, excused himself and went to talk to him.

Deborah stayed with me, motivating me to join the crowd. "Lissa, you need to enjoy yourself, it's party time!"

"I will, Deb!"

I looked across the hall and noticed that Randall's friend was tall, had a totally shaved bald head. He was hard to miss and he was looking directly at me.

"Deborah, do you know that guy Randall is talking to?"

"No, I never saw him before, but we'll know now... They are coming this way."

They approached and Randall introduced us.

"This is my friend Charles Hartsplend, my girlfriend Deborah and our friend Lissa."

"Nice meeting you, Charles."

Charles had a beautiful smile, I thought he was much more attractive up close.

Randall chatted briefly with him and then went dancing with Deborah again, leaving Charles and me alone.

Charles was eager to start a conversation. "I have seen you on TV maybe once, and I was impressed."

"Thank you, I'm not on TV often, I am not an anchor like Deborah, but I'm on the internet and in the newspaper..."

"Do journalists like to dance?"

"Sorry, I'm not much of a dancer, Charles, I hardly go to parties."

Like he hadn't heard me, he took my hand. "Come, this is an easy one."

He held me tight, I followed his steps slowly, and as we danced I started feeling at ease in his arms.

After that, we tried to find a quieter spot to talk.

"Lissa, I usually don't do this, but when I saw you across the floor I asked Randall to introduce us... I didn't come here tonight to find anyone, I came to have a little distraction and see a few friends, but first I should ask you... Are you alone? I mean, unattached?"

"Unattached, Charles, and I am glad we've met."

"How long have you been working in DC?"

"Only a year, I was with the network in Chicago before they offered me the opportunity to come to the Washington Bureau."

"That is when you met Deborah, I suppose. She is a big name in the news!"

"She is! And she is a big supporter of the newer journalists. I met her years ago when I came for an internship, since then we have maintained contact and became friends. What about you? When did you meet Randall? Do you work with him at the State Department?"

"We met ages ago when we were both deployed to Iraq, we were Marines. When we returned we both took advantage of education opportunities offered by the military right here in Washington. Randall ended up at the State Department, and I am at the Pentagon."

"The Pentagon! Are you with the CIA?"

"Sorry, Lissa, that is something I can't talk about, my job is Top Secret. That's all I can say."

"Oh, a secret agent… I know of those jobs, it might be very hard not to be able to comment on what you invest most of your time and energy in."

"It bothers the people around me more than myself, it becomes something in the way of developing closer relationships…"

"I understand and empathize with what you are saying, Charles."

We danced again, this time I was much more relaxed.

A little later Deborah approached us.

"We are going home soon. Do you want to come with us?"

Before I answered, Charles said, "I would like to take you home to continue our conversation…"

I hugged my friend.

"Thank you, Deb, I'd like to stay a little longer, I'll go back with Charles later."

Deborah whispered in my ear, "Randall told me he is a very good guy. Good luck!"

After they left, Charles took my hand. "One more dance?"

They were playing a selection of romantic songs. In his arms, dancing slowly, the melody and the lyrics felt suitable for that moment, and I got a feeling of familiarity…

'At last my love has come along, my lonely days are over and life is like a song…'

When the music was over we stayed still for a moment, holding on to one another, gazing into each other's eyes. I broke the silence.

"I've always liked that song made famous by Etta James, *At Last…*"

He smiled.

We left together. I gave him my address and he drove me home and parked in front of my building on Connecticut Avenue.

Without saying a word he looked into my eyes and kissed me, a long, loving kiss… Then he said, "I felt like kissing you right in

4

the middle of the ballroom, Lissa. That last dance was pretty romantic, and I don't use this word loosely."

I spoke the first thought that crossed my mind:

"To be fond of dancing was a certain step towards falling in love..."[1]

"Is that your quote?"

"No, it's Jane Austen's. I learned it from my grandmother..."

"I made a connection with you tonight and I'd like to keep our conversation going, unless you have some prejudice towards bald guys!"

I laughed, "Oh, that word follows me! No, I have no prejudice about anyone or anything, I find you charming, Charles."

"What about coffee around here on Sunday afternoon? I'd like to see you in the daylight."

"Do you think the spell might be gone after midnight? Sunday afternoon is perfect."

We kissed again. What a feeling! I would go on and on, but we said good night.

As I arrived in my apartment I sat quietly in the dark, I didn't want to wake up from a dream. I just met someone very special and I felt like never before.

Charles made a great first impression! Was it because he had a distinguished presence exuding confidence or because he was assertive? Am I making too much out of this encounter?

I couldn't sleep that night, I thought of my Grandma... I just mentioned her and a flood of memories took over me, I couldn't take her out of my mind...

***

During my early childhood I got the best of my grandmother, she nurtured and instilled in me an interest in reading, which led me to writing later on.

Grandma loved to read, and although I was only a little girl, she shared with me the stories she read and what she learned from them. She started reading them for me before I could understand what she was saying, but I was amused by her melodic voice, by her interpretation.

I was her only audience, my older sister didn't have any interest and my two brothers wouldn't stay still...

I was barely eight when she started reading *Pride and Prejudice* a chapter at a time. I didn't understand most of the words, like countenance, acquainted, obliged, intrepidity... and interrupted her quite often. Sometimes she would explain them and other times:

"I don't know this one, Lissi, but I'll look it up..."

"Bunica, what is pride?"

"Pride is a good feeling that you get from your achievements or for the accomplishments of others that you care about and you can feel the same way about the qualities that you have... Do you understand, Lissi?"

"I don't know, Bunica. Do I have pride?"

"You should, you are a very smart and pretty girl, you should be proud of yourself."

"Ah, I know, I am proud of you, Bunica, you read so well."

"Thank you, Lissi, I delight myself reading for you."

Grandma never called me Monalissa or Mona like the others, only Lissa, but she started calling me Lissi after the heroine in the book. It sounded sweet to me.

"And what does prejudice mean, Bunica?"

"That's hard to explain to a child, but it is like when someone has an opinion about a person that it is not based on reason or facts."

"Bunica, I don't understand."

"You will learn it, Lissi, in time. I'm tired now, I need to rest."

I did learn the meaning of that word all by myself, I still deal with it in my daily life...

Grandma Eden was Jane Austen's biggest fan. She would tell me:

"From reading her books I learned many words and about a time when women were only validated when they would find a suitable husband, not much different from what is happening around us here..."

She found phrases in Jane Austen's books and she would repeat them quite often, like:

"I declare after all there is no enjoyment like reading!"[2]

As I grew up without her I continued reading those books, and it was like having Grandma back in my life, listening to her voice in the pages and maintaining a conversation with her. I found it soothing to repeat those quotes, and surprisingly enough I can still apply them to daily events or circumstances.

More than anything, that's my way of keeping my Grandma's memory alive, I don't want it to fade away... Why should I?

Grandma was the most significant person during my early childhood, I can say with certainty that she was the only one that loved me.

"Think only of the past as its remembrance gives you pleasure."[3]

I wondered why Grandma didn't read me stories like Cinderella or Snow White, about princesses that met their princes and lived happily ever after... I heard about them from the other girls in school.

My Grandma would tell me:

"Sometimes there is not a happily ever after, I don't want to fill your head with illusions, I prefer to give you real literature and Jane Austen was so wise... She never married."

"Why, Bunica? Smart girls don't marry?"
"I will tell you about it when you grow up, Lissi."

My Grandma Eden Ramona, our matriarch, was born in America, but she was very proud of her origins, her parents migrated from Romania. She tried to teach me words of her original language, I only remember a few.

Bunica meant Granny, or she would call me *printesa*, princess, and her friends would call her *doamna*, which means lady.

Oh, she was a real lady, proper, always put together, her hair well coiffed, her dark dresses with white collars or a lace blouse, she loved lace, and always a pearl necklace. I don't have a picture of her, but this image never left my mind...

She didn't use any low words and did not allow them in the house either. She would tell me that she would give me the best education possible, she could see how much I enjoyed school. She would tell me:

"Education helps you become the best person you can be."

I never met her beloved husband, my Grandfather Petru, he died before I was born. Grandma talked a lot about him, he was a tailor, a craft that he learned from his father, and he was also a savvy businessman, he opened a men's store in Princeton, West Virginia and prospered.

He was a gentleman, much older than Grandma, he had been married before and lost his young wife in childbirth. Devastated by his loss he spent many years alone, thinking he would never marry again until his late thirties when he met her, Eden Ramona, a young and educated woman from the Ingleside neighborhood.

He told her up front that he did not want children, he was afraid of losing her, and it would only be the two of them for life.

According to Grandma she loved him so much that she agreed and married him, and for many years they were happy alone.

A decade into their marriage Grandma Eden found herself pregnant. They were both very afraid, he couldn't fathom the idea that he could lose her and the baby... But everything went well, and Angelika was born healthy and beautiful.

To Grandpa Petru's delight she looked like his side of the family. She became a Daddy's girl, and he bestowed on her his love and attention, spoiling his only daughter.

Angelika got away with everything she wanted, he enabled her, contrary to Grandma's expectations. She wanted her daughter to be educated, refined, appreciative of literature, but Angel, as they called her, didn't want anything to do with it. She abandoned school, and in her teens she became a party girl!

She was no angel!

Angel became hostile towards her own mother, calling her stuck up, saying that she thought of herself better than anyone else...

She was very young when she met Rufus Thoor, an audacious, muscular young man from the wrong side of the tracks. Grandma didn't approve of him, but despite all the opposition Angelika married him.

Grandpa Petru in his generosity gave them a manufactured, pre-fab house, and they set up in the mobile home park outside Ingleside. He helped them financially throughout their first years of marriage, and he was a loving grandfather to my older sister Miranda and my brothers Dylan and Darien.

After Grandpa's death, Angel, my mother, tried to convince Grandma Eden to move out of her spacious house into a smaller place to give her the house, but instead Grandma invited Angel, Rufus and the children to move in with her.

Sadly that was a mistake...

I was born in that house, and Grandma took care of me since birth. I was the closest to Bunica. Mira was six years older and hardly spent time with me, my brothers were very close in age, twenty months apart, they were always together. I was kind of the odd child and I was treated as such by my parents.

My mother was nothing like Bunica. She was full of vanity and would spend hours taking care of herself. "Looking good and attractive is a woman's job."

She only took Mira along on her shopping trips. Mira was her favorite, she never made any secrets. "Like mother, like daughter."

My father had a bad temper, he was angry all the time, I was afraid of him. He treated Grandma with disdain and contempt, sometimes he yelled at her, 'Leave me alone, old witch,' when Bunica told him to stop drinking or not to smoke inside the house.

Till this day I have an uneasy feeling thinking of him. I enjoyed the time when he was away. He worked in road construction and would take off with some other men in his truck for weeks.

Bunica and I had the best of times when he was not there. She let me sleep in her bedroom and would read me stories until late, sometimes she had to stop talking because she was out of breath, she had asthma.

***

I spent the night engulfed by these memories…

On Sunday afternoon I met Charles at a café nearby. He greeted me with a warm embrace. It was cold, he was all bundled up, wearing a nice gray knitted cap. "My mother knitted it for me," he told me while removing it. "It keeps my head warm."

"Why do you shave your head?"

"Because I started going bald really early, in my twenties. Instead of working with the hair I had left, I got rid of it, it's easier to keep it. I know it makes me look older this way."

"How old are you, Charles?"

"I'm thirty five, and you?"

"I'm thirty two."

"I'm glad we are in the same age range, we might have similar interests and goals in life."

"We might! I know you can't talk about your job, but what about your family? Does your mother live around here?"

"No, my family lives in Iowa, they are farmers. I left them when I joined the military, but I see them as often as I can. They are great people, I respect and love them. What about your family? You mentioned your grandmother the other night. Is she around?"

"No, she died when I was almost nine years old, I have no family left. And please, if you don't mind, that's something I don't like to talk about."

"That's fair, I can't talk about my job, you won't talk about your family. We have much more to talk about us, our experiences and goals, I just wish we had more time together, tomorrow I'm taking off on an assignment, I'll be away for a week."

"Do you travel often, Charles? Do you go alone?"

"Yes, often, most of the time we go in a group, but this time I can't wait to return and continue seeing you. Something really special happened when we met, almost like it was fate. When I saw you interviewing someone on TV, maybe a month ago, I liked your style, I was hooked, I thought you were so clever with your questions and witty in your comments, and I loved your blue eyes… I think we have something going for us. What do you say, Lissa?"

"I didn't expect to meet anyone at the ball, as a matter of fact that was the first formal ball I ever went to, and there you were. It was like when we meet someone and it feels like we know them already from another time, another life… I feel comfortable with you, Charles, and that is a big step for me, I am a bit of a loner…"

"What do you mean? Have you avoided close relationships?"

"Yes, I have, I have been on my own most of my life."

"You didn't have anyone special?"

"I did, of course, but it was not meant to be…"

"Tell me more about you, Lissa, you said you came from Chicago… Is that your hometown?"

"I am from Pittsburgh, Pennsylvania, but Chicago is a significant city for me, I went there for my master's in journalism and that's where I had the chance to start my career. I love Chicago, it is impressive, millions of people, the skyscrapers! I lived there for six years."

"I see you are a city girl! Why did you choose political journalism?"

"I didn't, just fell into my lap… I liked to write, and one of my professors directed me to an internship at a local newspaper, they had a vacancy in politics, and with time I learned to appreciate it. I started meeting all sorts of people, the egomaniacs, the narcissists, the philanthropists, the self-promoting and the ones that truly love people and are sincere about their purpose. It is interesting, enticing."

"From what I saw, you are good at it, I didn't see either commenting or interpreting what the interviewee was saying, and that is rare."

"I took my journalist's oath very seriously, I only report the truth of what I hear or see, I don't make up stories or offer my personal interpretation or judgments. Words are powerful, I write or say what I hold in my heart to be true."

"That's admirable, we need more of you out there… Sometimes I get disgusted by commentators, they underestimate the intelligence of the public. How did you get to be so wise?" He held my hand.

"Not at all, Charles, I have a lot to learn."

"And a lot to live. What about if we do it together? Learning, living, loving… I have been longing for someone like you. What do you think?"

"I had convinced myself that I was meant to be alone, I didn't want to be with anyone, but you are not anyone, Charles, and you touch a chord in my so far dormant heart… Yes, I would love to keep seeing you, I'm sorry you have to go on a trip tomorrow."

We sealed it with a kiss, and another and another…

As he walked me back to my building, he told me, "When I'm out on a mission sometimes I can't call, but I promise I'll maintain some contact, don't think I will forget you, and I'll come to see you as soon as I'm back. Will you wait for me?"

"Sure, I'll wait."

"Thank you for believing me, not everyone accepts this conditional, secretive job that I have."

"I need to believe, Charles, that there are truthful and honest men, I don't see any reason for you to deceive me, but I need to ask you… Do you have any other relationship? Anyone?"

"Of course not! The last committed relationship I had was years ago, and so far I haven't had any serious feelings for anyone until now." He hugged me, "I am looking forward to have much more time together." He gave me his personal phone number, "It will be off most of the time, but if you contact me I'll respond as soon as possible. And call me Chuck, that's how I'm known among my family and friends!"

I felt sad when he left, I wished I could hold on to him and ask him not to go. What's happening to me? I'm so independent, used to being alone, so far I didn't form a lasting attachment with any man... I am insecure and fear creating emotional ties.

I called Deborah on Monday.

"Deb, I had a surprisingly good weekend, Charles and I talked, and I really like him. Did Randall tell you anything else about him?"

"Yes, he said that Charles is a great guy, he was hailed a hero during their last tour, he saved a few lives. I think you got a good one! But I also want to invite you to come to my show on Friday, I'll send you the contents."

"I'll be glad to, thank you, my friend."

"I think him everything that is worthy and amiable."[*4]

I have lived a lonely life with very few emotional connections, denying myself a true commitment. So far the two loving relationships I had were to fail since the very start, I am sure that's the reason I started them, because I knew they were not going anywhere.

I carry a toxic guilt about the past that makes me feel undeserving of love, and I tell myself that I am fine on my own. Am I? In reality I have been treacherously unhappy and I crave closeness, love, family. Will I continue running from myself?

I am also feeling uneasy about what I have told Charles. There I was, telling him how truthful I am about my work while I have concealed from everyone the truth about myself, I'm afraid of others' prejudices or judgments.

During the next few days I got very absorbed by my job all day long, but in the evening, alone in my apartment, I felt overwhelmed by my childhood memories again... I have avoided reminiscing so far, for a long time, I feel uncomfortable remembering certain events of my early past...

***

One day a few months away from my ninth birthday, my father returned from one of his jobs out of town. Grandma was not feeling well, and he was drinking and smoking heavily. She asked him not to smoke in the house, he yelled at her:

"Leave me alone, old woman!"

"You forget that this is my house, Rufus, you are living here only because I don't want my grandchildren growing up in a trailer park. If you are not comfortable under my roof, you should leave!"

He cursed. He had a foul mouth.

She went to her room, I followed her.

"Bunica, I'm afraid of Dad. Can I stay with you?"

"Sure, Lissi, but please find my inhaler, I think I left it in the living room."

I went back. Father was watching TV and drinking, there were a few empty cans of beer on the floor, I tripped. He yelled at me:

"You are clumsy. Go away!"

"I need to find Bunica's inhaler."

"Just go, I'll bring it later if I see it."

"Bunica, I didn't find it, Dad said he'll bring it later if he finds it, but I brought you some cold water."

"Don't worry, Lissi, I'll be alright, rest, you can stay here tonight."

I helped her with her pillows, she was reclined on her bed, I could hear her wheezing from across the room. She couldn't read for me that night, I lay down on the loveseat and slept. I had the most terrifying nightmare.

When I woke up in the morning, there was a commotion and noise, my mother and father were shouting. Bunica was quiet, she was not wheezing anymore and her eyes were open. I came close to her:

"Bunica, are you feeling better?"

Father screamed, "She can't hear you, idiot, get out!"

He grabbed me by the arm and threw me outside the room. I hit the wall and fell to the floor.

I was hurting and stayed there, shaking and crying, *'Bunica, Bunica...'* I felt like I was falling into a black well and couldn't understand what was going on. But I soon realized that was the worst day of my young life.

Mother started making many calls, to the doctor, the pastor from our church, neighbors, friends. Soon our house was full of people.

The doctor came first, and the pastor told my mother he was taking care of everything for the funeral...

Then he came to me, "You were the apple of your grandmother's eye. Be brave, child." He held me up, "What happened? You are bruised!"

"I fell and hit the wall. I want to see my Bunica."

"You can't, child, your Grandma went to Heaven."

He asked my sister Mira to take me to another room. Nobody came to talk to me until my Grandma was taken away from the house.

I never saw her again...

Grandma never finished reading *Pride and Prejudice,* the book was still lying on her nightstand, I took it and hid it.

Days went by, and I didn't feel any better. My heart hurt so much, I cried and cried. My mother got upset with me and told me to never talk about Grandma again, especially in front of my father.

Life in our house went on like nothing had happened. My parents moved into Grandma's room, the best bedroom. They looked happy, Father bought a new truck, Mother got some new furniture, and they gave away all of Grandma's things.

By the end of the summer my father gathered Grandma's books to burn them in the firepit in the backyard.

I begged him, "No, Bunica loved her books, I'll keep them! Please!"

He hit me with a wooden stick, leaving marks all over my back and legs.

My mother took me inside, "I told you to never talk of her again." She gave me a towel soaked in cold milk, "Go to your room, make a compress."

I told myself that was the last time... He would never hit me again… But he did, many other times. That's when I decided I was going to run away far from him. I avoided being around him and became isolated and drenched in guilt feelings.

'Oh, if I only had found Bunica's inhaler, she still would be here…'

That same year around Christmastime my mother had another baby, the last one, a girl, Melinda, I fell in love with her. Melie became my baby, I was her primary caretaker.

Miranda was engaged and got married the next year. She married well, the groom's family had money, my parents were proud, they gave her a big party, she wore the largest and most glittery dress I ever saw, there was a lot of drinking and it ended up in a fight, which was very common in our family.

Mira moved to Martinsburg, West Virginia, with her husband Duke. I was impressed by his loudness and the enormous gold rings he had on his fingers.

In our community some of us would attend high school or go to college, and in our family we were allowed to stay in school until eighth grade. My parents would say that it was a hassle to go to the high school in Ingleside, we lived on the outskirts of Princeton, two miles away from Ingleside.

Most of the boys would go into the construction business with their fathers, and the girls were groomed to be wives and mothers.

I loved school, I was a good student, but I was told over and over that eighth grade was my last. I used to pray, *'Bunica, please help me, I want to go to school.'*

My father never treated me like he treated my siblings, he talked to me with pejorative or demeaning words, stupid, liar or worse. He said I was ugly, my skin was pasty white, my hair had no color, and that I looked just like my Grandma… In my heart I was proud of looking like her!

My mother told him she would improve my appearance as soon as I became a teenager.

I remember my heartbreaking graduation. While some of the

other girls and boys were going on to high school, others were happy for never having to go to school again. I held on to my teacher Miss Myrthes, asking her to do something for me to go to high school. She spoke to my mother, and in tears she told me she couldn't help me.

I never forgot her words… "I firmly believe in you, Monalissa, you'll go on, you'll find a way to attain your education, don't give up!"

I begged my mother to let me go back to school, I told her I did not want to get married at seventeen or eighteen like the other girls, I had dreams… She dismissed me and started teaching me how to be a good wife, to clean, cook, but most of all to always be submissive to a man.

She also changed my appearance. She took me to her hairdresser and had my long hair colored black. "Makes a better contrast with your blue eyes," she said, and also took me to the tanning salon.

She bought me tight-fitting clothes which I hated, I felt very uncomfortable in them, I didn't look like myself anymore. She told me that I looked attractive and was at the age of finding a husband.

On my sixteenth birthday they gave me a party! My very own, first party at a local restaurant. A lot of people came, mostly from our church. My father introduced me to Jesse, the son of his friend and business partner Vegas.

"I don't know why, but Jesse likes you, he is a good guy for you to marry."

"No, Father, I don't want to marry anyone, I want to go back to school."

"You are going to get married and leave the house. It's a done deal."

That night Jesse danced with me, he did not talk to any other girl, he told me he had his eye on me for a while, he said I was beautiful and tried to kiss me, I pushed him away, he smelled like alcohol and tobacco like my father, I hated that smell. He tried to hold me, I couldn't imagine being close to him. Marry him? Never! I told him I had no intentions of marrying anyone.

The next day I begged my mother, "Please help me talk to Father, I can't marry Jesse, I don't like him and I want to go to school, to college."

"There is nothing I can do, Mona, I agree with your father's decision. Jesse is a hardworking young man, he will provide well for you and he likes you, he thinks you are the prettiest girl he ever saw…"

Oh, I hated to be called Mona. My Grandma was the only one that used to call me Lissa. That was my name!

"This is not me, Mom, without this black hair and all the makeup and these clothes there is nothing left, he wouldn't even notice me."

"Obey your father, that's all I can say. You were always a rebel… Since the time my mother put those ideas in your head about books and education… She tried with me too, never worked…"

"Mom, you married my father against her will, she did not like him and you did it anyway. Why can't I? Why can't I go to school instead of marrying a loser?"

My mother slapped me on the face.

"Don't ever say that again!"

I became frustrated and went to talk to my friend Bessie, we were neighbors and best friends since first grade.

Bessie was also engaged and she encouraged me to obey my parents and get married.

"That's all we are meant to be, wives and mothers! Don't you like Jesse? Not even a little bit?"

"No, Bessie, I don't like any of the boys around here, I will not get married! I want to go to school, to get a job and become a professional, independent woman."

"But, Mona, girls like us do not have a chance out there."

"What do you mean? What's wrong with us?"

"I don't want you to go away, you need to conform to this life. I don't want to lose my friend!"

At that moment I thought Bessie was talking about the bond

that we had since childhood, when she relied on me to protect her against the bullies in school.

Bessie had a birth defect, a cleft palate, and she had difficulty pronouncing words, not everyone could understand her and the mean boys were always teasing her. I got in trouble in school for trying to protect her. Even after she had surgery and got much better, she still spoke with a nasal sound, she didn't like to talk much in public. I continued taking some of her assignments, like reading in front of the class, and that made us closer.

"Bessie, I understand, you are my best friend, and I don't want to be away from you either, but this is my life, I can't see myself married to someone like my father. I'd rather be dead! If I marry Jesse, I will never have the chance to go to school and become someone…"

"Mona, calm down, don't do anything stupid, it is not so bad. Don't you want to be loved and cared for by a man? And have your family? You love babies, I see how you love your little sister… Please just chill, it is going to be OK."

I could clearly see that Bessie, even being the good friend that she was, could not understand my situation. She was well loved by her parents and she was in love with Tony, her fiancé, and looking forward to marrying him…

From then on, my father got more aggressive and disrespectful with me, he humiliated me in front of Jesse. It was his way of intimidating me. That only made my hurtful feelings towards him grow.

I observed other fathers in our neighborhood treating their daughters like little princesses. I was never treated that way, and he would say quite often that I was not like his other children, I looked too much like Eden. My heart became filled with resentment and I couldn't call him Father anymore. I detached, in my head he was only my mother's husband Rufus!

Jesse would go out of town often with his father and mine on construction business, but as soon as they returned he would come to see me.

I learned to tolerate his way, he was tough but kind to me.

"Don't worry, Mona, I'll be a good husband, you'll be a happy wife."

I thought I could talk to him, "Please, Jesse, I'm not ready to get married, please be my friend, tell my father you don't like me anymore..."

"Are you kidding? If I don't marry you your father will find another guy, I want you all to myself..." He laughed at me. "Are you playing hard to get?"

Throughout that time I dedicated myself to my little sister, she was the only reason holding me back in that house. I became very depressed with the thought that eventually I would move out and I would have to leave Melie one way or another.

My mother started preparing my wedding, Rufus set the date around my seventeenth birthday. She took me to Princeton, to Sonja's Bridal, chose the dress, not as ostentatious as Mira's, but big and full of glitter, her style, not mine.

Three weeks before the wedding she had it all ready, the church, the hall for the reception. Jesse was out of town with Rufus, and I had the last fitting scheduled. The evening before, I went to my mother's room, sat on her bed and tried to talk to her calmly, "How did you convince your parents to allow you to marry Rufus?"

"I tricked them, my father adored me, he would agree with anything I wanted!"

"Alright, Mother, you got what you wanted, I won't play any tricks, but I am telling you I will not marry Jesse, I am running away. Father is a violent drunk, I want to be as far away as possible from him, from this life he put me through. I will not marry a man that he chose for me, with your help or not!"

I was determined, I surprised myself for being assertive, my mind was made up, she couldn't stop me.

I went back to my room, my heart broke for Melie, she was only seven years old. I read her a story, told her I loved her, part of me wanted to stay with her, but I couldn't renounce my right to be free from the oppression in that house.

The next morning I put my precious book and my birth

certificate, the only document I had, in my purse and left with my mother for the bridal store. When we arrived in Princeton she gave me eight hundred dollars cash to pay for the dress.

"I am going in alone, Mother," I told her firmly.

"Mona, listen to me! You won't have the guts to go away, it is a scary world out there, you are going to be homeless and will never be accepted back in our house. Anyway I'm going to the beauty salon and I'll be here by 2:00 p.m. to pick you up."

"Thank you, Mom." I felt like crying.

She didn't show any emotion.

I got out of the car, and she left.

That was the last time I saw my mother, the last time someone called me Mona.

I stood on the sidewalk for a little while, doubting if I should go. To the right I would get to the bridal store, to the left I would reach the bus stop two blocks away. My heart was racing, I was frightened, had no plan, I didn't know where to go. The only place I knew outside Princeton was my sister's house in Martinsburg, but I couldn't count on her to help me, she would return me back home immediately.

I knew I needed to get out of town. I turned left.

I arrived at the bus stop and took the first bus to Charleston, our capital. From there I could go by train or bus to another state.

I had been to Charleston once with Grandma on my eighth birthday to visit the public library, and that was my first and only time in a big city. I was impressed.

She had taken me previously to our local library in Princeton a couple of times when she promised me that every year, to celebrate my birthday, she would take me to other cities and other states to visit the most amazing libraries.

That celebration in Charleston was unforgettable. Grandma put me in my best dress and a big bow in my hair. I remember everything about that day, the bus ride, and my amazement when we got to Charleston and when I saw the enormous, beautiful library building!

Until this day whenever I go to a library, and I have visited them in all the cities that I travelled to, I have that joyous feeling of walking in my black patent Mary Jane shoes with Grandma holding my little hand and telling me with excitement in her eyes, "This is where you'll find all the books in the world that can teach you anything you want to learn!"

***

CHAPTER TWO

HOPE

*C*harles is back!

On Friday, after I taped the show with Deborah, I got a call from him. He was flying out of Heathrow, London and he would come to see me as soon as he arrives.

I was so excited, I met this man a week ago, saw him only twice, but I feel a strong connection. How is this possible?

He came on Saturday afternoon, and I invited him for dinner.

"You arrived from a long trip, I don't think it is a good idea to go out to a crowded restaurant."

He helped me out in the kitchen for a little while.

"You are right, Lissa, I do prefer to stay in, it's more restful and cozy."

He was affectionate.

"I missed you, I thought of you all the time. What did you do these days?"

"I worked intensely, also had many thoughts here alone, and yes, I missed you too, Chuck."

We had dinner, then we talked and talked. He said he would like to tell me about so many places that he visits in the world, but he can't discuss his work trips.

I told him I haven't been abroad, but since 2008 I have travelled quite often across the U.S., covering campaigns, debates, caucuses.

He mentioned among other things his preferred activities, sports, he is athletic.

"I'm not athletic at all, Chuck, but I like to go for long walks."

"We'll do it together," he responded.

He loves music, both classic and popular, and added he likes country too.

I put on some music in the background! We relaxed, holding hands, interlocking our fingers...

"I'm enjoying this phase of getting to know you, Lissa."

"Me too, Chuck, tell me more about your family."

"My family always lived on the farm, which is family owned for three generations, they produce soy. It's among the largest in the country. I gave them a very hard time when I decided to leave and join the military, I was obsessed with being a Marine. It was a calling! They worried about me, but supported me anyway. My older brother Colin stayed, working alongside my father, he lives on the farm with his family, a wife and two boys."

"Do you regret leaving them?"

"I know they suffered with my absence and I do regret causing them distress, but I do not regret living my life my own way. I want to tell you that before I was deployed the first time, I got married to my high school sweetheart."

I froze, "Married?"

"She was my first love, we were just kids, and I was going into the war not knowing if I would come back. But she gave me an ultimatum to return home or... After my second tour of duty she divorced me, she decided to go back to school and left. I had to accept it, I was so stressed out then, had been exposed to so much atrocity, but still determined to go back to Iraq. I went for my third tour."

"What happened when you returned, Chuck?"

"After I came back from the war I was an emotional wreck, I needed rehab, but my feelings for our country grew deeper in me and national security became my passion. I would be a frustrated farmer if I had returned to Iowa."

"I think your parents are exceptional, supporting your choices, not imposing their expectations on you."

"They are, but right now I want to place all my attention on you, Lissa, on us. Let's relax together, maybe watch a movie, or better..." He hugged and kissed me passionately, "Make out."

I went along with it, I was wishing for more closeness and affection. I have denied myself the fulfillment of those feelings for too long.

"Are you going to invite me to stay tonight?"
"Chuck, let's see where this will take us, give us time…"

The next day we went for a long walk out and about town.
"Are you going on a trip again soon, Chuck?"
"No, not for a month, we can spend much more time together. I might get us tickets for a concert or a play. Would you like that, Lissa?"
"Very much! I love to be in your company."

During the following month our relationship grew more and more, I got attached to Charles, enjoying being with him. I looked forward to our next date and the next…
It served me well, it was a tradeoff that he couldn't talk about his job, and I wouldn't talk about my family.

I met Deborah to discuss a project and told her, "Deb, I am in the most amazing relationship of my life, I am falling in love with Charles, but I am so scared!"
"Scared of what? He is a good guy, and you deserve to be happy, Lissa. Judging by the twinkle in your eyes, I can see you are in love!"
"We connected instantly, I feel happy with him. Before Charles, I didn't feel deserving of love, my self-worth and self-esteem had been damaged. This is a new experience for me."
"I wonder why, Lissa. What happened to you? You are a brilliant professional and an exceptional and beautiful woman. What's the matter?"
"As far as I can see, it is because I was not loved or validated as a child, but I came to realize now that I can't keep waiting for a day for all things to be made right for me. I have to work on myself."
"Have you had any romantic relationship before that made you question yourself?"
"I did, in Chicago. Something I am not proud of, I didn't think

I deserved better… But in the end my inner voice spoke louder and I let go, spending the next few years alone."

"Lissa, you need to overcome whatever happened in your past to give yourself a chance, or you'll never know."

"Someday I will share more of my history with you, Deb."

That conversation brought me back to 2009, when I was working at the newspaper and met Travis, an editor, a mature, charming, charismatic man.

It started out based on physical attraction and good chemistry, and deep inside I came to realize that I was carrying on only for the affection, to feel loved.

Travis was a great lover, but also a good liar… Initially he told me that he was separated, getting a divorce. Months later he confessed that there was no divorce for the sake of his children, blah, blah...

Because of my low sense of self-worth I went along with it for a while, I didn't think then that I deserved a permanent, solid relationship.

Days later Charles told me, "There'll be another trip coming up soon, but before that, I would like us to spend the weekend together. Would you come to my place, Lissa?"

I agreed, I felt like it was time to give us a chance to become closer.

Charles lived in Rosslyn, Virginia, right across from the Potomac with a great view of DC.

"And what is better, it's just five minutes away from the Pentagon," he said.

"I love the view, the river down below… It is pretty here."

His apartment was large and had a locked closet in the master bedroom.

"Sorry, this is private, no one can open it but me, it is my confidential office where I keep my computer and files from work."

"I understand, Chuck, I won't intrude on your job."

He had a romantic dinner prepared for us, and right after, he surprised me with music.

"I got it for you, for us, our song, *At Last*!"

We danced. At that moment, that melody belonged only to the two of us.

"That first evening when we met, you said something about dancing and falling in love... I have fallen in love with you, Lissa."

We let our passion take us into our first night of love.

"I'm in love with you, Chuck..."

"It is not time or opportunity that is to determine intimacy; it is disposition alone. Seven years would be insufficient to make some people acquainted with each other, and seven days are more than enough for others." *5

In the cold of the winter we had the warmest days and nights of closeness, and our relationship grew stronger.

We were not only dating, it was much more than that, I felt like we were embarking on a love story, but I felt afraid that I was not whole enough to sustain so much closeness and intimacy. Because of my insecurities I had a crazy impulse to put an end to it, but I couldn't, I was drawn to him.

'Would he still love me if he knew who I am?'

Charles went away on another trip somewhere in the world. In this divided world he deals with sensitive matters of peace and war. Is he in danger? It is hard not to worry! That is the price of loving someone...

I concentrated on my work, but at night, alone at home, my mind took me on a memory trip back to the past. I didn't know exactly what was happening to me, it felt like my brain was purging all that I had repressed or tried to ignore for so long.

Is this what happens when we love someone and we feel compelled to share everything? Maybe it was just guilt for not sharing my past experiences with Charles, and they kept coming up to the surface.

***

Back in 1997, one hour and a half after leaving Princeton, I arrived at a bus station in Charleston and decided to take the first bus going anywhere out of the state.

At the ticket office I was informed that there was a bus leaving for Cleveland, Ohio, in forty minutes. Without hesitation I bought a ticket.

There was a variety store at the station and I saw some sweatpants and tops, I got a large gray one with a hoodie, went to the restroom, washed my face of all the makeup, applied only a little lip gloss and put on the oversized gray top, pulled my hair into a bun and covered my head with the hoodie to disguise myself. I was shaking, felt like crying. I didn't know what to expect, being a runaway was terrifying!

I went to the platform and boarded the bus. The driver announced that it would be a ride of about eight hours to Cleveland, with a stop in the middle of the way for dinner. I took my seat and was happy that no one sat next to me.

After the bus took off I cried and held on to my book and prayed for my Grandma to help me find a place to hide where no one would ever find me.

During the ride I had mixed feelings. What was I doing? What if I wouldn't find a place to stay? My mother was right, it was a big, scary world, but I would not go back to my house, I knew exactly what kind of life I would have if I had stayed, and that was more frightening to me than adventuring into the unknown.

The bus went all the way up I-77 North until hours later, when it was already getting dark, we reached a stop at the intersection with I-70.

The bus driver announced that we were in Cambridge, Ohio and would be taking off in thirty minutes straight to Cleveland. Some of us would switch to another bus to Columbus.

I was hungry and tired and realized I had an option of going either way. I asked him if I could continue the next day. He said yes. I was terrified of arriving in Cleveland late at night, not knowing anything around.

Cambridge seemed like a friendly town.

There was a Walmart near the bus terminal. I went to the store and bought a few items of clothes, two boxes of hair color that I thought looked like my natural color, a pair of scissors, some toiletries, and walked across to a very large red sign that said 'Motel' with a diner attached to it.

I got some food and took a room at the motel. There were noises outside and I moved the dresser against the door. I heard a siren and froze.

'The policemen are coming to get me,' I thought.

No, they just sped down the road… I sighed in relief.

First I ate, I was famished, then I went into the shower and scrubbed myself hard and long, I wanted to remove the fake tan, I was hoping to look like myself again… But it didn't work, it just faded away a little. Then I cut my hair short, chin length, and colored it and washed it again… It looked terrible, almost like the end of a broom.

I finally slept with the lights on.

I woke up late the next morning. Before leaving the room I read a brochure describing Cambridge:

'A major interstate stop located in southeast Ohio on the Appalachian Plateau. The town is known for having a variety of glass manufacturers attracting interested collectors. It offers a National Museum of Glass, a Living Word Amphitheater described as a beautiful outdoor venue, antique markets, a Victorian Village and beautiful light and music displays at the Courthouse during the holiday season.'

Those were new things for me that I never heard or saw before.

It seemed like a nice town, so I decided to stay another day, maybe I could find a job there. What job? Who would give a job to a minor with no experience or references?

When I got out of my room, I saw that there was an enormous parking lot behind that area with many trucks moving in and out. I realized that it was a roadside motel mainly for truck drivers.

At the diner there was a handwritten sign by the cashier: 'Help

Wanted.'

"What kind of help do you need?" I asked the man who was preparing burgers.

"Someone to clean the rooms, do laundry and give a hand here at the diner, preferably someone that lives close by, but you need to be at least eighteen years old. Are you?"

"Yes I am, I just turned eighteen." I lied, I was about to turn seventeen.

"In that case talk to Clive when he comes downstairs. He is the owner."

I stayed around until Clive came, he had an apartment over the diner. He was the same man that I got the room from the evening before: short, with a big belly and not so friendly.

"Hi, I heard you are looking for help with cleaning and laundry, I can do that really well and I need a job."

"You look too young, girl. How old are you?"

"I'm eighteen, maybe I don't look like it because I don't wear any makeup."

"What's your name? Where are you from?"

I stuttered, "I'm Lissa from western Maryland, I don't have anyone here and I need a job and a place to stay."

"Are you a runaway? I don't want any trouble here."

"I'm no trouble, Sir. I just need a job!"

He measured me up, I felt uncomfortable. He thought for a little while.

"Let's see what you can do, we will give it a try starting now. I'll pay you minimum wage in cash, no paperwork necessary, if you know what I mean... I'll give you a room and you can eat here at the diner, but you have to pay for room and board, working another extra twenty hours a week... Deal?"

"Deal! Thank you, Sir."

"My name is Clive." He went back to the counter and got a key for room number nine. "You can move into your new room."

The cook called me, "I'm Grover, welcome on board. I'll show you what you need to do."

Grover was friendly, he had a big smile showing a gold front tooth and he wore a colorful cap hiding his dreadlocks. I felt I could trust him.

I started my duties working from 6 a.m. to 6 p.m. every day until Clive told me, "You do a good job, Lissa, better than I expected. You are hired! Grover also appreciates your help at the diner."

He paid me in cash. "You are off on Sundays."

'I got the job!' I sighed.

Cleaning was something I learned from my mother. She, like most of the other women, were very proud of maintaining the house shining, which we girls were taught to do from an early age.

There was a bus stop right in front of Walmart, I went downtown on my first day off and visited some of the spots I had seen in the brochure, I liked the downtown area. On the way back I stopped at Walmart for a few things.

The diner was closed, I didn't see anyone around until I got close to my room, a man approached me.

"What are you doing here alone, pretty girl?"

"I live here. Are you a guest?"

"Your guest maybe."

He grabbed me, I screamed as loud as I could and hit him with my shopping bag. He shouted some horrible words…

Clive heard me and came running.

"Leave the girl alone, you bastard, I'll call the police on you."

The man ran to the truck parking lot.

I had fallen and was scratched, I was crying.

"I'm sorry, Clive, I didn't do anything…"

"This room is a bit isolated, I'll give you the one next to the diner, I think you'll be safer there. And I'm not calling the police, I don't like to deal with them…"

"Me neither, Clive, I'll be alright. Thank you for helping me."

I was petrified that he would call the police and they would find out about me…

That night I thought of my mother, she told me it was a scary world. She was right, and I questioned myself.

'What have I done? Living miserably in a roadside motel, working like a slave, being attacked. Is this what I ran away for? How am I going to get my education?'

I cried myself to sleep.

On Monday Grover talked to me.

"Clive told me what happened last night, I still don't know what a pretty little thing like you is doing alone around here. Don't you have any family?"

"No, Grover, all I want is to go to college, I didn't even go to high school and I found out that there is a high school in town, but I feel that I'm too old to start and don't know what to do now..."

"Have you heard of a GED program? My son Maury got his certificate that way and now he is the manager for the copy and printing store downtown on Main Street, he can tell you everything about the GED, go talk to him, he never comes this way..."

"I'll go, thank you, I'll ask Clive for some time off."

"You don't have to, this one is on me, you can take a break after you finish your duties and go."

I got so excited thinking that was the solution to obtain a high school diploma.

That afternoon I took a couple of hours and went to meet Maury.

"My Dad called me and told me about you. I'm glad to help you with all the information you need."

He explained how it worked. I had to register at the training center located at the high school, I had to be eighteen, have an ID, study the assigned subjects, and in about two years do the tests to obtain the certificate.

I got discouraged.

"Two years? That sounds like a long time and I don't have a driver's license, I never learned to drive..."

"No problem, you can go to the Motor Vehicle Department and get a non-driver ID. In the meantime I can give you my old brochures and books, you can start studying on your own, you seem like a smart girl, you can do it."

He brought tears to my eyes.

"I don't know how to thank you, Maury, you are like your father, he is so kind to me."

"My father is a good man, he raised six of us working double shifts, flipping burgers, and he can't write or read, he only learned to sign his name, but he knows what is important in life."

I came back to the motel, optimistic and grateful.

Days later Grover brought me a backpack filled with papers and brochures.

"Maury sent this to you and said if you need help understanding, just stop by the store, he will help you."

Grover and Maury were the first good people that I encountered in the big, scary world. They gave me a hand with my quest for education. I will never forget them.

However, I did not tell them my real age and had to wait another year to get my ID and to register for the program.

During my first year in Cambridge I bought a dictionary, I read *Pride and Prejudice* again and again until I understood all the words. I also decided to buy other Jane Austen books, *Sense and Sensibility* was my first acquisition. That way, I felt I was keeping my Grandma's literary interest alive.

Reading was all I did for entertainment after working sixty hours or more a week.

On holidays I had my tea party for one, just like the tea parties that I had with Grandma when I was little. I would take a day away from food and only had English tea, shortbread, cookies and bonbons for dessert! And that made me smile.

Oh, good memories can take you a long way!

Sometimes I missed the familiarity of being around my house, I missed my little sister terribly, especially when it came to her birthday around Christmastime. I wondered if my parents had looked for me. It was a sad and lonely time.

I used to spend my free time or holidays alone, locked in my room, I always had my dresser against the door and I cried myself to sleep almost every night.

Looking back I know now that I was depressed, I was growing up in isolation, harboring self-defeating feelings.

I believed and came to accept that even my mother didn't love me, she grew indifferent to me and resentful of my Grandma, saying that she was teaching me to become stuck up like her... Mother facilitated my escape, she wanted to get rid of me, I was a misfit in the family.

During that time I never socialized, did not make any friends. But there was a man, a truck driver, Gavin, that came to the diner occasionally and started talking to me and asking me out. I avoided him, not surprisingly I was afraid of getting closer to him or anyone else.

One day he brought me a box of chocolates and invited me to a movie. I told him, "I don't go out with anyone, I am here only to work."

He didn't give up. I finally told Grover, at this point I felt I could count on him, and I was right. Grover spoke to Gavin and told him to leave me alone...

It worked. But then he asked me, "Why are you so afraid of getting closer to people? What's wrong with you, girl?"

I couldn't tell good old Grover that I was a minor, a fugitive, and afraid of being found.

One year went by and finally my eighteenth birthday came! I treated myself to some professional-looking clothes and dressy shoes that I bought in a nice department store downtown.

My skin was pale again and I asked the lady at the cosmetics counter for some advice on light makeup. She did more than that, she gave me a makeover, and I liked the way I looked.

As much as I was thrilled with being eighteen, I felt an overwhelming sadness for not having anyone to celebrate that special day with.

I remember looking at the mirror and seeing a reflection of my Grandma... I thought she would say, *'Happy Birthday, Lissi, I love you!'*

The sweet words she said were becoming a faint memory, it

had been ten years since she was gone. But I remembered when I was little and I couldn't recite prayers, my Grandma told me to speak from the heart and Heaven would listen to me, and I would feel comforted.

I prayed:

'Bunica, the world is not beautiful when we are not loved and alone...

The nights are darker and the howling wind rustles through the tall trees. It is frightening!

Bunica, I think of you and hear your voice in the books I read.

Can you see me? This is me, all grown up, and I am like you. I'll make you proud!'

By the time I enrolled in the General Educational Development program, I had already made a lot of progress with the material Maury gave me.

At the center, doing preliminary tests, they told me I could finish the program in another year. I was thrilled!

In one way it was discouraging to think I would spend another year scrubbing bathrooms, doing laundry, servicing raunchy people, but I was grateful Clive never asked me for a document to prove my age and paid me cash every weekend.

I was thankful I had a job and was able to save some money for what I needed to do next.

Once Grover told me, "I'm sure you'll leave us after you get your certificate. You're going to do something better than this."

"I hope so, Grover, I am going on, I'll find my way to college..."

A few weeks before my final tests I started noticing a man that would come in a white delivery van almost daily. He called himself Joe. I don't know why, but I didn't have a good feeling around him.

The first time I offered him some coffee he responded, "I don't want any coffee, I need a fix."

I didn't understand him.

"What do you mean? This is not decaf, it is regular coffee."

He laughed out loud, "You know what I mean!"

"I'm sorry, I really don't, but I'll ask Grover."

As I was turning to the kitchen, Clive approached us.

"I'll take care of this customer, go on, Lissa."

I left as they started a conversation and told Grover, "I don't know what that customer wants, I hope Clive doesn't get angry at me…"

"No, he won't, let him deal with it."

A couple of days later Joe came back.

"Call Clive for me, please, I want to talk to him."

I went upstairs and knocked at Clive's door and told him Joe wanted to talk to him, he told me to send him upstairs… I thought it was odd. Clive had friends that sometimes would go up, but I never saw him inviting a customer to his apartment. Anyway Joe went upstairs.

I finished my work and went to my room to study, I had my finals coming up in a few days.

The next evening I went to the testing center for practice. When I returned, as soon as I arrived at the bus stop in front of Walmart, I could see several police cars with lights flashing right in front of and around the motel. I had no idea what was happening and got extremely distressed.

'Maybe somebody robbed the cashier…' I thought.

I worried, all my things were in the motel, my books and my final tests to complete… I ran across the street and asked a police officer, "Please, can I get my things? I live and work here."

Immediately he put handcuffs on me, forced me into the back of a police car and told me, "We are taking you to the Police Department downtown."

At that moment my world collapsed, I couldn't even speak. In two other cars nearby I saw Grover, and in another, Clive. Grover was looking at me with despair in his eyes. I mouthed to him, "What's happening?"

They drove us to the Cambridge Police Department and put me in a cell alone. I sat in a corner and cried, not understanding what was going on. Later a female officer brought me something to eat and a blanket.

"It's going to be a while until they talk you. Eat and relax."

"Relax? I don't know what is going on. Why am I here? I didn't do anything."

She did not answer and walked away.

I might have slept a couple of hours, the officer came back.

"Freshen up, Officer Alvarez is going to speak to you."

I rinsed my face, arranged my hair with my fingers. She put me in handcuffs again and guided me to a long hallway into an interrogation room.

Officer Alvarez came in. What a shock!

"Joe!"

"I'm not Joe, I'm Officer Alvarez."

I broke into tears, I couldn't stop crying, he removed my handcuffs, gave me a cup of coffee.

"Relax, everything has been sorted out, and I know and the Department knows you have nothing to do with it, but I still need to ask you a few questions."

"I don't know what's happening, Officer, I have no idea."

"How long have you worked at the motel? Did you witness any drug deals taking place?"

"I have been working at the motel for over two years. Drugs? I never saw anything."

"Well, I needed to confirm you were unaware. Clive kept you out, and by doing that, he protected you."

"Clive was fair to me, he gave me a job and a place to stay. Besides working really hard he never expected anything else from me. What about Grover? He is so hardworking and kind, I can't imagine he is in trouble…"

"They are both in custody, I can't discuss it with you. What I wanted to say is that, doing a background check on you, we realized you were a minor when Clive hired you, and you had no documentation. Did he know?"

"No, I lied to Clive and he never asked me for an ID. Am I in trouble for lying about my age?"

"No, but tell me the truth… Are you a runaway? I saw in your ID that you are from West Virginia, I ran a check but didn't find any missing person's report on you."

I started crying again.

"They never tried to find me… And during all this time I did everything to keep in hiding… What's going to happen to me now? Do I have a police record?"

"No, you are free to go, but I suggest that next time you find a better place to work and live."

"I am only days away from completing my GED, I want to go to college, that's why I ran away from home, I was not allowed to go to high school. What do I do now, Officer?"

"I am a father and I can't imagine not offering my children every single opportunity of education. You will finish your GED and then I suggest you move on, go to college. We are going to give you your money back, you can build a life for yourself."

"My money! I saved it from my work, Clive always paid me in cash."

"I know, he told us, we had to confiscate it… You need to open a bank account, you should not keep money in a drawer. And after you complete your tests, come to see me here at the Department, maybe I can help you decide what to do next."

Officer Alvarez gave me an address of a hostel in town where I could stay for a few days, he also sent me back to the motel with another officer to collect my things.

I stayed downtown for another week, completed and passed my tests and visited Maury in the store. He was devastated, he couldn't believe his father was involved with the drug deal.

I also saw Grover and Clive in jail, I thanked and wished them the best outcome.

Grover cried, "All I want is to go back to my family." My heart broke for him.

I came back to the police station to talk to Officer Alvarez. He asked me if I knew what I was going to do next.

"I want to go to a community college to prepare myself for a university, but first I need a job, I am not sure if I should stay here in Cambridge."

"I have a suggestion in case you decide to move out of this

area. Years ago a relative of mine moved to Pittsburgh, Pennsylvania in search of education and better job opportunities and had a great start there."

"Thank you for the suggestion, Officer, I'm thinking I should move on."

He offered me an address of a place to stay in Pittsburgh.

"Monalissa, allow me to give you some advice... You are a pretty determined and smart young woman, you have no reason to keep your head down. Lift your head up, look people in the eye, don't be shy. You are strong, you know how to fight for what you want and you are going far in life. This is a father's advice that I would give to my own daughter."

I became emotional, I lifted my head and looked into his eyes, and I saw a good man with the best of intentions.

"Thank you, Officer Alvarez, your daughter is a very lucky girl to have you as a father."

"Shyness is only the effect of a sense of inferiority in some way or other. If I could persuade myself that my manners were perfectly easy and graceful, I should not be shy."[6]

From there I went straight to the public library and did research on Pittsburgh. I loved what I saw and made my decision! I wanted to experience life in a large city.

I was just a girl when I arrived in Cambridge, I knew nothing about the world, I grew up in loneliness and fear. During those years I tried to obliterate my origin and my past, and I became resilient and determined to reach my ultimate goal of going to college. I left as a grown up with mixed feelings of achievement and sadness.

To Pittsburgh I went, carrying my precious books, an ID, a Social Security card and an equivalency certificate that I attained at age nineteen! I did it!

It would have been so much easier if I had someone to share my life with, someone to love me, to hug me and to say that they were proud of me. Someone!

From my new book I learned these phrases that held meaning about myself and inspired me:

"She was stronger alone..."
"I will be calm; I will be mistress of myself."*7

***

Charles called me on arrival from Dulles Airport!
I felt happy, he is back again!

"Oh, Chuck, I had no idea how much I could miss someone that I have known just for a short time..."
"I couldn't come any faster, Lissa, to hold you, to pick up where we left off. You put a spell on me! I can't take you out of my mind."
In his arms I felt so happy, I just wanted to love him, love him.
"Please don't go on another trip anytime soon..."

"Her heart did whisper that he had done it for her."*8

Our relationship kept growing fast and deeper. We were always together.

Spring came and it was beautiful. Washington was entirely in bloom, crowded with tourists coming out of their winter cocoons.
I enjoyed the cherry blossoms so much more this year on our long walk at the Tidal Basin... All the cherry trees in full bloom of pink, delicate flowers reflecting on the water and small petals dropping on the sidewalks like snowflakes... Enchanting!
Then after having a delightful dinner at a trendy new place, we went home to cozy up. Charles' favorite thing to do...

"Lis, tell me more about your life in Chicago before you came to DC."
"During my master's I was offered an opportunity to intern at the local media network, which I enjoyed very much. After completing my program they offered me a permanent position at the political bureau.

My writing style was appreciated, they labeled it 'The Regency Period.' I dared to throw in some old, eighteenth century English words and some quotes, and they thought I was giving a fresh spin on hard political talks. I made a name and grew as a professional.

I also became independent, finally having my own place, and most of all, I enjoyed the life of the city.

During that time I was assigned to a temporary internship on Capitol Hill.

My first time in DC! I was fascinated, what better place to be for politics than Washington, DC.

After six months I returned to my job and started travelling all over the country. It was a thrill! But I loved to return home to the Windy City.

Finally in 2012, much sooner than I could have predicted, my boss offered me a position in the DC Bureau, the senior reporter in line for a promotion did not want to relocate his family, so it was offered to me. Initially I didn't like the idea, I was established in Chicago, but then I thought it was a great professional challenge and I came."

"That's all? You only talked about your work. What about your personal life? Did you leave any important relationship behind?"

"I didn't have anyone important in my life in Chicago at that time."

"It puzzles me that you do not talk about your close relationships, maybe someday you'll trust me enough to tell me."

"Chuck, it is not about trusting you, it is all about me. I buried many of my previous experiences, it causes me pain when I revisit them... I shut down my feelings, but yes, I had a few close friends, some are still present in my life."

"Can you share those with me?"

"I left a couple in Pittsburgh, I worked and lived with them until I went to the University. They helped me throughout my years in school and beyond, I'm still in contact with them. The last time I saw them was in Chicago, months before I came to DC, when they came to fly to Russia. They went back to Sochi to buy an inn, that was their dream. They are happy there, we are in touch mostly by postcards now."

"I heard Sochi is a nice place. Do you plan to visit them?"

"Yes, someday, they invited me to come, and I truly would love to see Olga and Igor again."

"That's all? What about a love interest? Anyone in Pittsburgh?"

"Yes, my first love, but he had to move away to follow his family's expectations. What about you? Do you still think of your first love, your ex-wife?"

"Sometimes, there was never resentment between us. I have seen her parents, they still live in the town close to our farm. Meghan lives in Iowa City with her husband and children. But don't change the subject, Lis. Did you have any other loves in Chicago?"

"As you can see I have avoided intimate relationships, but I had one in Chicago that made me reformulate my values. I went along with it for a while, justifying to myself that I would never have a commitment anyway... The truth is I didn't feel deserving of a loving relationship, I felt inadequate."

"From what I see I think your family had a lot to do with the way you felt about yourself. Do you want to talk about them?"

"I lost contact with them sixteen years ago and during those years I made the biggest effort in forgetting them... But I'm coming to terms with it and eventually I will tell you more. I owe it to myself to be true, to not have hidden issues."

"My darling, I know that someone in your past, most certainly during your childhood, hurt you badly, that's why you didn't feel deserving of love. When the day comes and you want to open up, here I am, not only for the good times, I want to share it all with you, all that you are, all that I am.

I wonder about you. What happened? Were you abandoned by your parents? Did you grew up in foster care? I wonder... But know that no matter what happened, I see you as you are, loving, caring, a very competent professional, and as the icing on the cake, you are beautiful, and I love you, Lis!"

"Oh, Chuck, thank you for understanding! I love you."

We hugged! How comforting it is to be in his arms! I have never been so much in love like I am now...

The next day he started talking about his family farm. How

42

magnificent it is there at this time of the year.

"Why did you leave your family, Chuck?"

"No specific reason, I had a wonderful childhood, had everything that a boy wants and enjoyed the farm life, the thousands of acres of fields of green crops, the rolling hills, I enjoyed nature, the horses, everything!"

"You had a nice family, a girlfriend. What attracted you out of there?"

"I was restless, I wanted to see the world, and after we got a visit from a military recruiter in high school, I felt it was my duty to fight for my country. My other option was to go to the School of Agriculture and Land Stewardship in Des Moines, I was not motivated…

My parents were devastated but did not stop me from enlisting, they let me make my choices, for which I am very grateful."

"How are your parents now? Do they talk about you coming back?"

"My father sometimes mentions that he would like me to take over the executive and administrative responsibilities. Colin, my brother, is the farm man, an expert in cultivation, he has extensive knowledge of the land, he could teach me much."

"Do they work alone? Or do they have help?"

"They have plenty of help. My father leased some parcels with their own managers. They have thousands and thousands of acres of soy plantations, it is an enormous enterprise."

"That is! What about your Mom? Does she work along with your father?"

"Mom is very active, she was a social worker, she is always involved with the workers' families. She is a great support to my father and also keeps my grandmother company."

"Grandmother! How lucky you still have your grandmother."

"And she is incredible, almost ninety years of strength, energy and love!"

"Chuck, after you came back from the war, why didn't you feel like returning home?"

"I was emotionally distraught, I needed treatment first, then I became more invested in my career in national security. Honestly I do question myself sometimes… Why didn't I return home? My family deserved that. Maybe it was because my marriage failed and I thought I had nothing to go back to? I dealt with it and here I am. Things happen for a reason…"

"I am glad you are here, Chuck, we had the chance to meet."

We didn't talk about the past anymore and we continued spending all the time we had available together, loving, laughing, enjoying a good movie, sharing common interests, like couples in love do.

There is closeness and warmth, honesty and passion between us that I haven't experienced before… And that frightens me, there is a risk that my heart could be broken.

Charles was going on a trip again…

"This time I am allowed to mention that I will be away for ten days, starting in Eastern Europe and continuing to the Middle East, but I won't be alone. Kevin, my partner in this project and my friend, is coming too."

"Oh, Chuck, there you go again, I feel apprehensive but at least I know you won't be alone. How long have you worked with Kevin?"

"A long time, since I got this job, he was there before me. He is a good friend, I'll introduce you when we come back. He and his wife Suzy live in Arlington, not far from here."

"I'll be glad to meet your friends."

"You'll like them, Suzy is a lovely woman and they have two children. They are living proof that married life is not incompatible with our line of work."

I thought to myself, *'Was that a hint about married life?'*

*"[She]… told herself likewise not to hope. But it was too late. Hope had already entered…"*9

And with that, Charles left on his trip.

CHAPTER THREE

MY OWN WAY

*F*eeling lonely I have retreated into my thoughts again… There is a certain urgency in me to put the pieces of my life together. I have much to overcome, hiding emotions and memories hasn't helped me at all!

***

I was in awe of what I saw when I arrived in Pittsburgh. At the bus station I took a cab to the hostel Officer Alvarez had recommended.

The cab driver was very friendly and proudly described some of the landmarks of his city.

"Pittsburgh is one of the most visited metropolises in the U.S. and it is the largest city in both the Ohio Valley and Appalachia. And it is located at the confluence of three rivers! The Allegheny, Monongahela and Ohio."

He also mentioned that Pittsburgh is known as Steel City or the City of Bridges.

All of those bridges painted in yellow made a big impression on me.

It was beautiful! Just like I saw in pictures.

With so many buildings, businesses and industries I first thought it should not be difficult to find a job, but then came reality: What was I qualified for?

I had spent the last two and half years cleaning rooms, doing laundry and serving at a roadside diner, and only had an equivalency certificate. In a city with so many colleges and universities, that didn't mean much… But I tried.

I put on my best professional suit, held my head up and went to a few hotels, looking for work at the front desk or maybe in reservations. But soon I learned that most of those positions were part-time and they gave preference to college students. I didn't qualify for that.

One of them offered me a position in housekeeping, but the salary was so low, I would not be able to afford rent. And how would I pay for my classes?

I got discouraged thinking that I needed to go back to the same kind of job I had in Cambridge.

I learned how hospitable and progressive Pittsburgh was during my search and long walks through the city, and about distinctive neighborhoods surrounding downtown, and experienced the most beautiful and unique skyline. Breathtaking!

A week after the defeating job search, I went back to Allegheny Community College to ask about registration for classes and was informed that, first of all, I needed a permanent address.

I explained to the clerk at the Admissions Office that I was trying to find a job and a place to live, but so far I had been unsuccessful. I asked her if she had any suggestions. Maybe I could apply for a job on campus…

She patiently heard me and then told me that Allegheny was one of five in the Pittsburgh area, there were another four community colleges that I could explore in the surrounding area, where maybe employment could be easier to find. She suggested Butler County College. She was very kind and gave me directions.

"It's a short ride, less than thirty minutes." She added that there was a golf resort in Butler County that I could look up, "They are always hiring, good luck!"

With my hopes up I immediately went to Butler. There, another helpful clerk told me that I could register if I had an address to start classes immediately. Gladly I learned that the tuition was a little lower than in downtown. The program would prepare me to transfer to another college or university in two years.

I liked what I saw! I told her I was going to find a job and I would be back soon for enrollment. I was determined.

As I walked down the road to get a bus to the resort, I saw a sign: 'The Sochi Lodge.' It was a small, two story building, very well kept.

'It is kind of a nicer motel,' I thought. 'I would work here, so close to the Community College, I would do any work, even if it is cleaning...'

I went in and asked the lady at the front desk if they needed any help. She had a strong accent, hard for me to understand at first, and responded, "I wish we had someone to stay at reception, greet guests, receive merchandise, answer phones..."

"I have worked at a busy motel and a diner in Ohio for over two years, I can do this job and I also like to attend to customers and guests. Are you the manager, Madam?"

"My husband and I are the owners, I am Olga. What is your name?"

"I'm Lissa, nice meeting you, Olga."

Olga called her husband, Igor, and he said he was about to post an ad on the Community College bulletin board. They had just lost an employee and he wanted someone to take care of reservations, do office work and eventually help inside when needed.

He also mentioned they lived on the premises and they both worked there around the clock.

I was hopeful and wanted to give them the best impression, I needed that job.

I understood they needed help right away and made a compelling plea, told them I needed a place to stay in that area, I was going to take night classes at the College nearby and that location would be perfect for me.

Olga started asking all sorts of questions: how old I was, where I was from, where my family lived... She looked very interested in knowing more about me. Igor stood there, observing.

I told them, "I am nineteen and a half years old, I came from Cambridge, Ohio for better education opportunities and I have no family."

"What do you mean?" Igor asked. "Are you an orphan? Or one of those foster kids?"

"You can say that." I was afraid I was giving them a bad impression...

Igor and Olga left me alone for a little while, then he came back and told me, "My wife and I are considering giving you the job on an experimental basis. We never had any employee living on the premises, but you seem like a responsible girl and you want to go to school. We might help you, but you'll need to work hard for that, it is not free boarding."

"I will, I won't disappoint you. Thank you for the opportunity."

Olga showed me a small room upstairs. She told me, "To pay for this room you'll need to do some extra duties, like folding laundry and organizing the closet supplies, the vending machines. I work all day and can't stay on my feet for too long."

"I will help with anything you need."

I moved in the next day and started right away. Igor told me he was planning to add a computer for reservations and other services, but he didn't know how to deal with it. I was honest and told him I didn't either.

"I'm going to take a class about computers, I will learn it quickly, I can do this, Igor!"

He gave me a letter confirming my permanent address to bring to college. "Education is very important, I want to see that you are really going to classes!"

Olga and Igor were a middle-aged couple from Russia, they had no children. They made no secrets in telling me that they wanted to make enough money to go back to Russia, the Sochi area, where they were from, and buy a property there and live happily ever after...

They had a dream and a goal, and they worked very hard for it.

Igor did all the maintenance work, and Olga supervised the cleaning crew and took care of the laundry. They were the hardest working people I had ever seen.

I went to a bank down the street and opened my first account. The assistant manager taught me how to write a check, gave me an

ATM card and made me sign up for a credit card. I felt like a responsible adult!

I started classes and one of them was on computers and technology twice a week. The instructor was a young man, a computer engineering major from the downtown university, Sunjay. His last name was so long and had so many consonants, I could never pronounce it.

He was a genius, I thought! He knew everything, had an answer for every question and was very patient. Adding to that, he was handsome, great black hair and a beautiful smile.

Sunjay bestowed a lot of attention on me and one evening he offered to walk me back to the Lodge.

He told me he liked me, he wanted to see me, but that was something forbidden for him. His family would never approve of a relationship with an American girl, he was Hindu.

"In our culture we respect and obey our elders and we follow the traditions."

"I like you too, Sunjay. Believe me, I totally understand family traditions, I am not the typical American girl and I don't expect you to not respect your parents and your culture."

I appreciated his honesty and started seeing him with no expectations. I was craving love and affection and I was attracted to him. As a matter of fact Sunjay was the first young man that I wanted to get closer to.

In the meantime he taught me everything about computers and he even helped install the programs on the Lodge's computer. Igor was so grateful, I became the computer expert, and neither he nor Olga ever had to deal with it.

Sunjay was my first love. My feelings for him were strong, I couldn't hold them back. Many times we cried because we knew we wouldn't be together for long.

One of the things that kept me with him is that he never probed me about my family. That subject was out of bounds for both of us, and I felt very comfortable with it.

I continued taking other courses at the Community College and he helped with other subjects too. He always praised my writing.

Months into our relationship Sunjay introduced me to his friend Bimal, who also had a secret American girlfriend. Sometimes we went out together with Bimal and Jenna, a very nice college student, and we became friends while enjoying our double dates in downtown Pittsburgh. The more I knew the city, the more I liked it.

Jenna had different expectations than I had. I told her that I loved Sunjay, but I knew that our love affair was not to last... She had hopes that she would end up marrying Bimal and they would live happily ever after.

Working with Olga and Igor was rewarding but exhausting, sometimes until late hours or on weekends, but they treated me as if I were their family and praised me quite often.

Sometimes Olga would bring me beetroot soup, *borscht*, at night when I returned from classes. At first I was afraid to eat it and have red cheeks like Olga. *'Maybe she eats too many beets,'* I naively thought. My face never got red, and I learned to love the soup.

I used to call Sunjay, 'my Sun.' He was the light of my life, and with him I felt warm and loved for the first time...

On a spring break he organized a trip for us with Bimal and Jenna to Philadelphia. We, the two young couples, had a wonderful time together, and that was my first memorable adventure in the largest city in Pennsylvania, the City of Brotherly Love.

We had the greatest time touring around, visiting the Museum of Art. The boys especially enjoyed running up those steps, the Rocky Steps, they said.

We had the chance to see the symbol of America's independence, the Liberty Bell, that is owned by the city, among other historical sites.

The four of us were in love! Young love! Like it would never end...

I was getting closer to celebrating my twenty-first birthday! It had been four years since I left West Virginia...

"Sun, I feel like I am an adult for a long time, but now I am officially becoming one. I have heard of people who changed their names, I read a story about it. Do you know how to do it?"

"Why don't you like your name? You never want to be called Monalissa, it's a classy name."

"It is, but I want to be Lissa, like my Grandma used to call me, and I don't like my last name Thoor. How can I change it?"

"It is easy, you go to the courthouse, file some forms and explain why you want to change it. What name do you want?"

"Doresc, that was my grandmother's family name."

Sunjay took me to the courthouse. I filed forms and wrote a heartfelt explanation for the request of the name change, paid a fee and waited a couple of months.

The day I got a notification in the mail to come to the courthouse to swear in my new name, my heart was about to burst of joy. I was breaking ties with my father's name, honoring my grandmother, and that made me happy!

Sunjay was with me that day as I raised my right hand and officially became Lissa Doresc!

To celebrate the event Sunjay gave me a pair of stud earrings! "They are very small, but they are real diamonds, Lissa. They will last forever, like my love for you."

"Thank you, Sun, this is the first jewelry that I received as a present from the man I love, I'll keep them forever."

I needed to continue at the Community College for another semester to take extra credits before applying to the University. Sunjay guided me through the process, suggested I apply for scholarships, and said he couldn't wait to see me getting my college diploma.

One morning a few weeks later he came to the Lodge, which was very unusual. He was distressed and disheveled.

"Something horrible has happened, Bimal was killed in a car

accident last night, a drunk driver... I lost my friend, I am devastated, his family is hurting so much... You need to help, Lissa."

"Oh, Sunjay, I'm sorry, so sorry, he was my friend too. What do you want me to do?"

"Go to Jenna and tell her not to come, she has to keep the secret, his parents are devastated enough, they shouldn't know their son was hiding that relationship from them, they should never know. I'll come and see you after everything is taken care of, I mean the funeral ceremonies... "

My heart broke, I realized in that moment that my time with Sunjay was about to end. He had a clear revelation of how our relationship would affect his parents if they ever knew.

Olga stayed at the reception desk, and I went to give Jenna the sad news.

Expectedly she was shocked, angry, hurt, she screamed and cried. I held her, "You can't go to see him, Sunjay explained that it would add to his parents' pain if they knew of you."

She screamed even louder, "But I love him and he loved me..."

I hugged her, we cried together.

It took a while for Sunjay to come back to see me. When he did, he was circumspect, looked older than his twenty three years... I took him to my room, it was our last time together, he held me...

"Lissa, I will always love you, but I can't be with you. I am promised to marry the daughter of one of my family friends. I'll be moving to northern New Jersey, where they live, and I've already applied to complete my Ph.D. there.

I'm sorry I have no choice, I have to fulfill my destiny. After I saw Bimal's parents suffering his loss I understood what a son means to his parents. They lost him, lost all the future that he would have, the life he would have built, his future children... I understood how my parents would suffer if they would lose me..."

"I understand your commitments with your family and your respect for your heritage. Sun, you brought love into my life like I never had before. I love you, I'll miss you and I'll keep the best memories of you. You never lied to me and I always knew we would have to part someday… But it hurts to see you go, it hurts so much!"

I went through a period of deep sadness and I shut my heart down. For years to come I would not have another relationship, believing that I would never love anyone like I loved Sunjay... No one would ever love me again...

"The more I know of the world, the more am I convinced that I shall never see a man whom I can really love."[10]

Olga brought me many servings of borscht. "You need to eat, girl!" That was her way of showing me that she cared.

I also saw Jenna often, we bonded over grieving for our lost loves. Jenna went from crying all the time to becoming cynical.
I thought that was what grief can do to a person… She started saying that I was in a worse situation than her.
"At least Bimal didn't leave me to obey his parents… He loved me and he was going to marry me no matter what."
"Jenna, Sunjay told me otherwise, Bimal was going to follow his destiny, that's what they do. In my case I feel comforted that Sunjay is living his life and I wish him happiness."
"I'd rather have Bimal dead than knowing that he would marry someone else."
"That is morbid, Jenna."

At the Community College I was involved with the school publication. One of my professors praised my writing, "That's the way you should go, Lissa!" I agreed, math and science were challenging subjects for me.

I finally got the good news I was accepted to the University in the fall. It was a thrill! More than that, it came with a job offer on campus with tuition remission and housing.
The campus was far from the Lodge, and I would have to attend day classes. I had to make a difficult decision.

When I told Olga and Igor, they were disappointed that I had to leave, but I promised I would find a replacement for my position, which I did, right there at school.

During those months Jenna made a startling decision, she was going to move to Florida. She failed her finals, did not graduate and declined professors' recommendations to complete her assignments during the summer to graduate the following semester. Instead she decided to leave and asked me to come along.

"Come with me, Lissa, let's start a new life! Palm Beach is a great place, you will love it! There are plenty of nice resorts and hotels, also rich men available for us to meet. We can have a great time and forget all the heartache."

"I can't, Jenna, I am going to the University in the fall, I worked so hard for it, I won't miss this opportunity, I still have two and half years to go... And you shouldn't miss it either, you are about to graduate!"

"I don't care about graduating, I want to enjoy life! You would come with me, Lissa, if you were a true friend, we have shared so much pain, now we should enjoy the good times... We'll find some rich guys there and have a much better future than here..."

I saw Jenna leaving that summer, she insisted until the last minute, I felt sad to lose another friend and worried about her, but I wished her well.

About a month later I received a postcard from her:
'Look at this sandy beach! Gorgeous, isn't it? I am having a blast, met a guy and we go boating often, I am having so much fun!'
And I never heard from Jenna again...

Olga cried when I left, I did too.
"Olga, I have been here in your house for almost three years and you have been like a mother to me, I promise I'll come to visit you, and in my time off I still can help you here if you need."
Igor and Olga agreed. "The door is open for you, come always." Igor gave me a bonus check as a present.

I had a hard start at the University... I was not the typical college student, young, carefree, I was older than most of my peers, my life experiences didn't match theirs, I felt mature beyond my twenty two years.

I kept mostly to myself, working, studying, learning with enthusiasm, and I was soaring. I worked in the Department of Communications with Professor Malvaney, she became a mentor to me, and I developed skills writing about the news, current events.

I did maintain my friendship with Igor and Olga and visited them quite often. I became a surrogate daughter and they invited me to stay with them for the holidays. It was heartwarming, like having a family, but knowing that it was temporary, eventually they would leave too.

During those years I was not interested in close relationships, I didn't form any romantic attachment. It was a lonely time, but I was used to being alone anyway.

In my second year I started feeling a sense of belonging among academia, professors, instructors. That environment never intimidated me.

Finally I graduated at almost twenty five years old and proudly wore a cap and gown. I couldn't speak and cried when I was called on stage to get my diploma. That was the culmination of my efforts. I did it!

On that unforgettable day in May, I knew I was starting to live the life of professional achievement and success that I dreamed of for so long...

I was ready to leave the renowned city of Pittsburgh to complete my master's to pursue a career in journalism in Chicago, one of the largest cities and one of the most important business centers in the country!

I was very excited, I was going to fly for the first time!

My only guests at the graduation were Olga and Igor, I was

grateful for their presence, their support and friendship. My dear friends!

"But remember that the pain of parting from friends will be felt by everybody at times, whatever be their education or state."[11]

***

When Charles came back we spent most of the time together. I have missed him so!

He told me that Kevin rents a house in North Carolina for two weeks every summer, and he invited us to come.

"He and his wife want to meet you, Lissa."

We went to Pebble Beach for a long weekend.

Charles was excited with the fabulous golf course by the water, "That's why I love coming here!"

I truly enjoyed meeting Kevin, Suzy, and their young children, Kev Junior, six, and Emma, a three year old doll!

I spent time with Suzy and the children while Kevin and Charles went to the golf course.

She told me that she was from Texas, and every summer after they spend time at the beach she goes to Dallas with the children to see her family.

"Did you meet Kevin in Dallas?"

"No, after I graduated in international studies I had the goal of pursuing a diplomatic career and I wanted to come to Washington, DC to make some contacts. My father was friends with the Texas State Senator and he arranged an internship for me at the State Department. For an entire year nothing came of it. I spoke to the Senator and he offered me work in his office on Capitol Hill. That's where I met Kevin, he was in the Secret Service. We immediately connected, and I decided to stay in DC.

We dated for two years and we are married for seven now, I gave up any idea of having a career to be home with my children. It is the most rewarding and challenging job, to raise a family."

"I believe it is! You seem like a happy couple, Suzy."

"We are, Kevin is a wonderful husband and father. He is also a great friend and he always wanted Charles to find the right person too, and from the way he looks now, I think he found it! It is obvious that he is in love with you, Lissa!"

"And I am in love with him! It was instant, there was nothing I could do but to love him."

"Did Charles tell you that I used to tell him that it was about time for him to find someone special?"

"No, he did not."

"Kevin told me he was lonely and out of luck, and I kept teasing him… I thought Charles would hate me for that."

"He doesn't, he told me you are lovely."

"You need to come to our house in Arlington, Lissa, I like talking to you. I really like to maintain contact with my professional friends, you are so current and updated on what's going on, I like to be well informed."

"Likewise, Suzy, I like your company and I'd love to come to see you."

I could foresee becoming close friends with Suzy and Kevin, I really liked them and enjoyed their company.

"My idea of good company… is the company of clever, well-informed people, who have a great deal of conversation; that is what I call good company."*12

Charles and I had an amazing time under the sun, relaxing, loving, with no worries in the world. Life was perfect! I told him that I had never seen the ocean until I started travelling for the 2008 campaign and went to Florida.

"Living always in the Midwest all I had seen were rivers or lakes. I had been to some fabulous beaches by Lake Michigan when I lived in Chicago, but it was not like the ocean."

"We'll come back here anytime you want, maybe once again before the end of the summer."

As fall arrived Charles told me he had to go to Iowa.

"I haven't been there since last Christmas. My family includes me in everything and I didn't make it to the Fall Festival, now I need to go for Thanksgiving. Would you like to come with me, Lis? My folks would love to meet you."

"Did you tell them about me?"

"Yes, of course they know about you and me."

"Chuck, I am so sorry, I can't take any time off, I'll be the only one covering the Bureau…"

"I see, maybe next time."

Charles showed his concern.

"Lissa, I sense there is something else, you have been secretive. I believe that a close relationship with secrets is unsustainable."

It felt like a blow, he knows me better than I thought, and I felt awkward.

There he was, telling me about introducing me to his family, but he really doesn't know about me… I owe it to be true to myself and to him! All I could say in that moment was, "I'm sorry, Chuck!"

I became withdrawn after that conversation, and during his absence I felt horrible. I was invited for Thanksgiving at Suzy and Kevin's, but I declined and spent four days alone, thinking and rethinking that what I needed to tell Charles would probably end our relationship…

Charles came back on Saturday and asked me to join him in his apartment.

"What's the matter, Lis? Are you upset because I went to Iowa? I couldn't miss the occasion, but I am here for our first holiday together, and next spring will be Grandma's ninetieth birthday, I told her you'll come then! Won't you?"

"Chuck, before you left we had a conversation about keeping secrets… All my life I have been withholding information about myself, avoiding situations in which I would feel compelled to disclose them because of my own feelings and prejudice towards myself. I have been living in conflict between telling the truth and being afraid of being labeled or misjudged.

I intentionally did not want to deceive you, we have a deep emotional connection and you deserve the truth.

I'm true to myself, but I carry secrets that erode my soul, it is like a burn in my heart. Because of that, many times I feel like a fraud, inauthentic. What I believe and practice in my professional conduct, I haven't applied to my personal life...

I do love you, Chuck, and I want our relationship to last, but I'll understand if when you know the truth about me you will walk away..."

"Lis, let go of the fears, free yourself. One of the first things you told me when we met was that you didn't want to talk about your family, it was obvious to me that something went wrong in your past... Tell me what I need to know, stop running away from it."

"Yes, it is about my family. My other fear was that as I start recounting old events, disturbing memories will impact me again..."

I walked to the large front window of his apartment and looked at the water down below on the Potomac River glistening under the lights and accepted the fact that this could be the last time I contemplated that beautiful view.

The world looked still and quiet, but my heart ached, our relationship could end tonight...

Charles came and put his arms around me.

"It's so beautiful outside, I feel so good with you, Chuck, I wish it could always be like this."

He was serious, held my hand. We sat together and a wave of calm took over me, I took a deep breath.

"I was born in Princeton, West Virginia, and I ran away from home three weeks before my seventeenth birthday. My name was Monalissa Thoor... My family was and is part of a Gypsy community. I am Gypsy!"

"Gypsy? You mean a real Gypsy?"

"Yes, for many generations. Mother, father and siblings, we are all Gypsies. My mother's side of the family came from Romania. My father's were Irish Travellers."

"Did you leave them just because they were Gypsies?"

"No, not at all. There is nothing wrong in being part of the Gypsy culture. There were many good families around there, but mine, unfortunately, was very dysfunctional."

"Why did you change your name and where? Tell me everything, Lis!"

"I changed it in Pittsburgh when I was twenty one years old. My Grandma always called me Lissa and her maiden name was Doresc, I wanted to honor her and cut ties with my father's name.

My Grandma was the only person in my family that loved me. She died too soon, and after that, my life with them became unbearable.

There was much violence at home, verbal and physical abuse. My father was controlling, didn't believe in education and did not allow me to attend high school. To top everything he arranged a marriage for me, I ran away three weeks before my wedding. I couldn't live the rest of my life with someone he chose for me, I had dreams, I wanted to go to school and be independent."

"What about your mother? She didn't support you?"

"No, she agreed with everything my father did or decided."

"How devastating, you have been alone since you were seventeen! And you went to school and to college, you did it all by yourself! You had the courage and strength, it could have gone so wrong, and look where you are now. I am amazed!"

"Thank you, Chuck. Looking back the only regret I have is that I left my little sister Melinda, I loved her, but I could not take her with me."

"Of course not, you were a child yourself. How did you get to Pittsburgh? Did you know anyone there?"

"No, first I went to Ohio and I lived in Cambridge for two and a half years, working at a roadside motel where I faced hardships and loneliness, there I started and completed my GED.

Then I moved to Pittsburgh, where I found a job at Olga and Igor's Lodge, and I went to the Community College before the University. I lived in Pittsburgh for over five years. I was almost twenty five years old when I graduated."

"I am astonished! I thought I had faced many challenges in the military, but you had a war of your own to fight all alone. You were a little girl! I'm so sorry, Lis."

"Aren't you horrified that I am not a real American girl? That I didn't have a good upbringing like you? I am Gypsy! *Zingarese!*"

"What is *zingarese?*"

"That is a term that refers to the original Gypsy style of music, ardent, vibrant, colorful. In my old neighborhood they would use that word often to refer to the Gypsy style of living of the ones that were itinerant, travellers, not settled permanently.

Ironically, of all my family I am the true wonderer, the errant, justifying my moves from state to state in pursuit of jobs and education... And that is something that makes me uneasy, I have a deep longing to create roots, to be permanent."

"I can understand why you had to move from place to place, that doesn't make you an unsettled person, but you should have told me before...

Anyway, I do not hold anything against you because of your origin... I see you as the intelligent, strong woman that I fell in love with the moment we met. Now I admire you even more, you are a fighter!"

"I never told anyone, you are the first to know, and I thought you were going to dump me when you knew the truth. Oh, Chuck, I love you, I do love you! I am sorry I didn't tell you before, I was insecure and afraid of stereotypes and prejudice."

"And talking about stereotypes, hum, I always thought of Gypsy women as sensual and seductive. You sure put a spell on me, Lis..."

"Somewhere inside of me lives a girl full of passion. You haven't seen nothing yet, Chuck..."

I kissed him like never before, we loved one another with endless passion, I could not believe I had all that fire contained in me for so long...

"You are the man I want to spend the rest of my days with. You are my forever, my love."

That night was all about our passion.

The next morning...

"Lis, when you feel like it, I want to know everything about your family, your culture. Were your brothers and sisters not allowed to go to school either?"

"They didn't demonstrate any interest in school. My sister Miranda was six years older than me, we hardly spent any time together. My brothers were very close in age, they were rambunctious and very attached. None of them ever argued about school, they didn't care. I was the odd one.

My father blamed my grandmother, saying that she had put those ideas in my head. Grandma would tell me that if it depended on her I was going to get the best education possible.

In my community many of the youngsters would continue in school and some eventually left for jobs elsewhere, that was not uncommon, but a few like my father were adamant about preserving their traditions and not allowing the children to go their own way."

"That's tragic, he limited the lives of his own children."

"Rufus was ignorant and stubborn, his way or no way! He was aggressive, sometimes brutal, he would call me pejorative names, would kick me or punch me, I was terribly scared of him. I still feel uneasy remembering and talking about him, my heart starts racing and I feel stressed out and anxious."

"I can understand, it is still very traumatic. You can tell me everything in your own time, I am here for you. In the meantime I'd like to suggest that you seek psychological help. I had it myself after the war, I think it is imperative for you to heal from your childhood trauma."

"I am sure you are right, Chuck. I always thought I could deal with this on my own. In this moment I have a sense of relief and gratitude for opening up to you."

"Go for counseling, darling, you are going to see how much better you will feel, you deserve it, Lis. When you feel like it, I want to learn more about the Gypsy culture and your experiences after you left Princeton."

"I can tell you right now, Chuck!

The Gypsies originated in India and later become nomads travelling through Europe, where they appeared in the fifteenth century.

They came to America two hundred years ago during the migration. Some came from England, they are called Romnichals; others from Eastern Europe, the Roms; from Romania, the Ludars; and also the Irish, known as Irish Travellers.

Initially they scattered mainly in the Appalachian states, with a concentration throughout West Virginia. But each group had its own historical tradition and some still maintain a social distance from one another.

For Gypsies keeping their culture alive is very important. They usually follow a law code that governs their conduct and lifestyle, maintaining their distinct cultural identity.

There was a clash of values right in my family. My maternal grandparents were Ludars from Romania and they lived by their own principles.

My father Rufus Thoor, a loud Irish Traveller, didn't discuss his history, and we never met a person from his family. We only knew that he left his community in Georgia when he was a teenager and went from state to state until he settled in West Virginia in a trailer park. He had nothing by then.

I believe he had issues with where he came from, he never referred to any relatives. It was obvious that his anger, disdain and contempt for others came from his past experiences, but I had and don't have any interest in digging into it. If my mother knew the root of all evil, she never disclosed it to us."

"What attracted a girl that came from a better family to a man like Rufus?"

"Maybe because Angelika, my mother, was too young and rebellious, maybe it was lust. I don't know.

Rufus didn't respect her family, he used to say that my Grandma 'had her nose up in the air.' In other words she thought she was better than anyone else, 'her kind was the best,' for that reason he wouldn't tolerate her.

With time, in that house I realized that he was not a typical father, he was a bully, always angry, drank too much and had no respect for anyone. He was not well liked even among his peers, he was belligerent and would start many fights, mostly with the Gorgers. That's how they refer to the non-Gypsies."

"What about your mother? Why didn't she follow your grandparents' traditions and marry someone like them?"

"She was a spoiled only child, her father enabled her. He died before I was born and my parents moved into my Grandma's house, she is the one that took care of me since birth. My mother resented her even more so because I looked much like my Grandma and nothing like her…"

"That made you the odd child. Now I understand what you were saying."

"I was very attached to my Grandma, and my parents hardly paid any attention to me, not only did they not support my interests like learning, my father resorted to abusing me verbally and physically with brutality."

Charles held me.

"I'm so sorry, Lis, that sears a little child's soul and leaves scars... Now it is time to heal!"

"As a little girl I wished I belonged to another family, I saw so many of our neighbors being loving and kind to their children, supporting their interests, and fathers that treated their daughters like little princesses. Especially after my Grandma's death I had the feeling that I didn't belong there, that's why I closed off, thinking that I was not worthy. My self-esteem was damaged, but somehow I gathered all my strength and fled."

"You did the right thing. You achieved what you wanted, we found each other, you belong with me, we belong together. So what should I call you... *Gypsy* or a *Gorger*?"

"Well, I was born and raised Gypsy, but because I fled now I am considered a traitor."

"I will call you *gorgeous*, that's what you are, Lis!"

Telling Charles my history was extraordinarily liberating. Contrary to what I anticipated my revelation brought us closer.

Charles is an exceptionally understanding man, he lifts me up, with him I feel capable of everything... His strength, his good heart inspires me. I can't see my life without him.

My fears of loving him are gone...

"I wish, as well as everybody else, to be perfectly happy; but, like everybody else, it must be in my own way."[13]

The holidays came around, and I attended an end of the year party with Deborah at the network. I told her that my relationship with Charles was amazing.

"Never been so happy in my entire life!"

"I feel happy for you, Lissa, enjoy this moment of your life while it lasts... I don't mean to be a downer, but the truth is that while your relationship is growing, mine with Randall is fading away... I will tell you more later."

"I'm sorry, Deb, you are a terrific friend and woman. I wish you the best, my dear friend, and I'd like to tell you something that

I kept a secret until now, you have been my best friend, you deserve to know."

"Now you got me curious! What is it? Something juicy? What about lunch tomorrow?"

"Lunch it is, Deb."

My friend Deborah is in her late forties. She has had a few relationships that didn't work for her, starting with an early marriage succeeded by two devastating miscarriages, ending in divorce.

She told me, "I was young and filled with dreams and hopes and I had to reformulate my expectations in life after I realized that everything is temporary and I was not meant to have a family of my own. All I want now is a true companion to share my older years with."

The next day I met Deborah and I told her everything about my origin and my earlier challenges.

She was surprised, "It must have been hard to conceal it from everyone, Lissa, mainly when you were still a teenager and alone."

She thought I had an interesting and unusual story to tell and suggested, "You should write a book. Writing is healing!"

"I agree, maybe I will someday! But what is happening to you and Randall? You looked so happy together, Deb!"

"I think it just ran its course. I have been very realistic about us, Randall is much younger than I am, he aspires to have a family and he should have at least the chance to try. I always knew we had no future together, our love affair was not meant to be. That's life! Next time I'll find someone my own age with the same expectations that I have."

"You will find love, Deb. You give love to the ones around you and you'll get it all back. That's a given!"

Charles and I had to work through the holidays, but we had a loving time together. We had a dinner party with Kevin and Suzy, and being in their house, warm and beautifully decorated for Christmas, with their children overly excited, anticipating Santa's arrival, made me feel that I have always missed having a family.

I have one good memory of Christmas with my family when Melinda was born. She was so cute, a living doll! I was so happy, she was the best present!

'What happened to my baby sister?' I still regret abandoning her... I feel so guilty.

On Christmas Eve I asked Charles to go to a special Mass at the National Cathedral. He thought it was a little odd, we never discussed or demonstrated religious interest, but he came with me anyway. It ended up being a great occasion with a magnificent choir.

That reminded me that I was part of the choir in college, I loved to sing, I feel like singing again... I had enough of crying, now it is time to be happy!

Charles called his family on the farm in Iowa on Christmas Day. They had a pleasant and long conversation, and he gave me the phone to talk to his mother.

It was the first time that I heard Magdalene's voice greeting me sweetly:

"Hi Lissa, it is so nice to talk to you. We all want to meet you, please come to see us soon, our home and our hearts are open to you."

I felt accepted as part of her son's life.

Charles planned to celebrate our first anniversary in January, in his apartment, a party for just the two of us. He prepared everything and he sounded ceremonial.

"Lis, there is something I need to talk to you about. We are seeing each other for a year now, we spend a night here in my place, a night there in yours, and during part of this time I felt like you were holding your feelings back, but not anymore. I love you, Lis, and I want to make our relationship more permanent. I want us to live together. I am asking you to move in with me."

"Together, Chuck, every day, every night!"

"Together for always! But I need to warn you that due to my position at the Pentagon I have to disclose who I am associated with and they will run a background check on you. Demands of this kind of government job..."

"A background check?"

"They need to be sure that the person that I'm sharing my life with has no criminal history."

"Chuck, I love you, and yes, I want to live with you, for always. You and I, it seems like a dream!"

Dancing to our song, we celebrated the first anniversary of our relationship and started the year of 2014 united as a couple.

CHAPTER FOUR

IN TIME

As soon as I moved in with Charles I found a psychologist specialized in trauma, hoping that it would help me get over painful memories and repressed feelings of my childhood, to be able to build a better life and a future with the man I love.

But as I started talking and answering her questions, I was having unsettling flashbacks, nightmares and a strong sense of guilt, sometimes despair took over me.

In the sessions Dr. Aldrin explained to me that as a small child experiencing trauma we could expect two outcomes: one would be disassociation and withdrawing into depression, and another would be pushing away visual memories and emotions caused by troubling events until they were forgotten, apparently...

It looked like my young brain chose the latter behavior, but it came with a price: misplaced guilt.

We had long conversations, and after much hesitation I agreed that in terms to have my life resolved and free myself from those conflicted feelings, I had just one choice... to unveil it!

"Where so many hours have been spent in convincing myself that I am right, is there not some reason to fear I may be wrong?"[*14]

I did discuss it with Charles and thanked him for his support.

"I thought I was going to feel better right away, but the contrary is happening. Thank you for standing with me, Chuck, I couldn't do this alone."

"Darling, you have suffered for too long, it has to be over. I understand that every family has issues, some worse than others, it is human nature to have disagreements... But they need to be resolved."

"Chuck, are there any conflicts in your family? It seems so perfect!"

"There is nothing perfect, there are unresolved issues between me and my brother, perpetuating some tension between us..."

"Do you want to talk about it?"

"Growing up Colin and I were very close, we did everything together, competed in the same sports and had the same life plan of going to agriculture school in Des Moines and continuing the family farming tradition. I looked up to Colin, he had a natural love for the land, and since he was very young he was committed to continuing in our grandfather and father's footsteps, making the farm grow and prosper. But he also had an interest in knowing more about the world and planned that in the future he would take occasional trips across the borders of Iowa and the country.

I was the boisterous and adventures one, always looking for thrills.

Colin was in college when I graduated from high school and decided to enlist in the military. My parents were devastated and he totally disagreed with me, saying that was not our family's plan. We were raised to stick together.

I left aware that I was not only leaving a hole in my brother's heart, but making my parents concerned about my well-being. I knew that despite being far away I was constantly on their minds, and when I went to Iraq I became the main focus of my family's attention. Colin stood on the sidelines, finishing school and later taking on his responsibilities, hoping and wishing that I would return home.

Every time that I visited my family, I was treated as a hero, but it still didn't move me to return and I chose to stay in Washington.

Colin witnessed our parents' anguish and disappointment for not sharing a life with me and my lack of interest in working with them.

They remained silent and never demanded that I would return, but Colin didn't make any secret of how he felt about my choice and how much I hurt my parents. He also told me that he felt neglected, he was the only one there, renouncing a life of fun as a young man to support our father, he thought his hard work went unnoticed.

Later when he married Kristin and moved out of the family home, he thought he was going to be able to start taking vacations with his wife and fulfill his longtime dream of getting to know the world. That never happened…"

"Chuck, I can see why he was resentful of you. Did you try to make amends?"

"I acknowledged what he said, that's all. Anyway, our rift had started years before in high school when we both fell for the same girl, Meghan."

"What? You both had a crush on the same girl? That couldn't work well between brothers."

"It didn't, Colin was a senior and I was a junior, Meghan was in one of my classes. We started going out in a group, but pretty soon she and I hit it off. He was upset. After his graduation he went to Des Moines, and when I graduated and enlisted, Meghan was very upset with me, and Colin had his hopes up…

About two years later when he was already back at the farm, working with my father, and I was about to be deployed for the first time, I decided to marry Meghan and took away his hopes that he would have a chance with her… I recognize how immature that was of me.

Meghan stayed with her family in town, but when I returned she demanded that I quit the Marine Corps. I didn't and went back for my second tour of duty, that's when she divorced me and moved to Iowa City.

The next time I was back home before my last tour, Colin was pretty mad at me. He said I messed up Meghan's life, his and my parents' lives, and nobody was happy with my choices. He told me I was being selfish and ego-centered. We had an ugly fight, I couldn't take back the consequences of my decisions. I felt I was living below their expectations."

"Chuck, do you think those feelings limited you from returning to the farm?"

"Sometimes I feel that way and I keep telling myself that I have this very important job that matters to so many, that impacts peace in the world, to prove that I have made the right choice…"

"What about Colin?"

"I saw Colin putting his life together, he tried a few

relationships until he met Kristin, she was a new teacher in town, and they became a happy couple. I am happy for him, but every time I go back I feel that he still holds a grudge."

"Does Colin talk to you about this?"

"No, but when I am there he still shows anger towards me, he feels that I come back and my parents roll out the red carpet and treat me with affection that I don't deserve..."

*"Angry people are not always wise..."*15

"Chuck, the day will come when you need to have a heart to heart conversation with your brother. You have a wonderful family, you are both grown men, don't allow that bond to be broken, it is hurtful to all, including you, I am sure."

"Lis, here you are, telling me not to break the family bond when you had reasons to break yours, you had no other choice, but I did and I do. Colin is my only brother... I'll make it up to him."

"Did you ever apologize to your parents?"

"Yes, I feel sorry for the distress I have caused them."

The more we talked and spent time together, and the better I knew Charles, the more I loved him!

Charles and I visited Suzy and Kevin a couple of times that winter.

"I am glad you and Charles are together."

"So am I, Suzy, he is the love of my life."

"I know that the job they have is very challenging, but with time you get used to it. In a way it is good that they can't talk to us about their assignments, that gives us more time to talk about ourselves."

"Don't you get upset when Kevin travels and you don't know where in the world he is?"

"Not anymore, I just wait for him to return home and make up for the time we spend apart. It has been seven years, I'm pretty used to his absences and his secret missions."

"What about the children? How do they deal with it?"

"Kev Junior whispers around, 'My Dad is a secret agent' and Emma is too young to understand."

Sure enough Kev Junior came to me and whispered, "Do you know my Dad is a secret agent?"

I whispered back to him, "That's cool!"

"That is the best attitude you can take, Lissa, it's cool."

"When Chuck goes away I get anxious and restless until I hear from him. How do you deal with that, Suzy?"

"Honestly I'm so used to it, I don't worry anymore, I'm busy with the children, in no time he is back! Charles told us that your job is very intense too, isn't it, Lissa?"

"Pretty much so, I have a lot to keep my mind busy."

I got a new friend and planned to visit her when Kevin and Charles go away. Together we'll have some girl time.

Suzy taught me a lot about the neighborhood and showed me the best places to shop. She also told me about her family that lives in Texas, she is the only daughter, her brother lives there, close to their parents, but her mother never gave up the idea of Suzy moving back home.

"Maybe someday when Kevin retires from the Pentagon, we can go and have a great life there. I like this area, but there is no place like home…"

A bond between Suzy and me has been formed, and I can clearly see that being married to a 'secret agent' is not bad after all.

Charles asked me, "Are you seeing that our job, as demanding and secretive as it is, doesn't stop us from having a family life?"

He hasn't said anything about getting married, but since we have been living together, I have nurtured this idea.

"Chuck, was that a hint?"

"Yes, I have thought about it. Haven't you, Lis?"

"I have, I want to be with you forever…"

We didn't speak any more words, we smiled and kissed! Life is promising now.

This spring was even more beautiful than the last, with an explosion of green of all shades all over the landscaped landmarks.

I appreciate and love this time of the year in Washington, DC, the City of Trees!

I learned when I moved here that the city preserves the richest diversity of trees, more than any other capital in the world. This is a living legacy of our nation's Founding Fathers!

In Charles' company, walking together, holding hands, everything takes on new colors, contemplating the beauty profusely displayed around the Tidal Basin, the cherry trees in full bloom of millions of delicate flowers! The falling petals paving the sidewalks like soft pink snowdrops... What a beauty!

When we are in love, everything looks more beautiful.

In May Charles reminded me:

"Schedule time off, we are going to Iowa, I told my folks that you are coming along to celebrate Grandma Tori's ninetieth! They can't wait to meet you, Lissa."

"I'm looking forward to meet your family."

Charles and I flew to Cedar Rapids. From there he rented a car and drove less than one hour to his family's farm. I was astonished with the endless extension of lush green fields, looked like a picture.

"It's hard to imagine during the winter how green it looks in the spring and summer, and how many tons of soy come from these fertile fields."

"I didn't expect anything like this, Chuck, it's magnificent!"

We stopped in the town close by, he showed me his former high school. There are about six thousand people living in town, but students come from all over the farmland.

We reached the farm, "Welcome to Splendland."

A long stretch of road led us to a large main house. In the middle of a plateau to the left, there was another house.

"That one is my brother's house."

He parked in the circular driveway and stopped by the front porch.

"There they are. Remember they like to be called by their first names."

His father Douglas and brother came out to greet us.

"Welcome home, son, and Lissa, I am so glad to meet you!"

His brother Colin was cordial and invited me inside.

"Go in, Lissa, I'll bring your luggage."

Magdalene, his mother, was at the door, waiting for us.

"Come in, Lissa, welcome home."

She hugged me warmly.

"I'm so glad to meet you, Magdalene." I was feeling shy, I was not used to warm family welcomes.

Once in the house I met Kristin, Colin's wife, a lovely woman, maybe just a couple of years older than me and a mother of two preteens, Ryan and Josh, Charles' nephews.

"Our boys will be here shortly, you'll meet them."

And there she was, Grandmother Victoria, Douglas' mother, a friendly little lady, about one hundred pounds of sparkle. She looked liked Charles described, spunky, sitting in her rocking chair.

"Come here, Lissa, I want to see you up close."

I came to her, "So nice meeting you, Mrs. Hartsplend."

"I'm Grandma Tori to you and to all, Chuck told me you have blue eyes like mine and that you are sweet and smart like me, that is why he loves you."

Everybody laughed. "I'm glad, that's a compliment, Grandma Tori."

Charles brought our luggage to our room upstairs, a suite.

"I thought they were going to put us in separate rooms."

"Why? This is my room and they know we live together, no problem, we farmers from Iowa are very progressive people."

"Indeed! And very welcoming too."

I came downstairs, and Douglas started talking about politics, asking my opinion about an array of candidates.

"You know them up close, don't you, Lissa? So what do you

think of them?"

"I'm sorry, Douglas, I won't talk about my personal opinions or impressions, I only report the facts I hear or see…"

"But you have feelings and preferences about them, don't you?"

"I sure do! During this next two years I'll be working closely with them and I will have a lot to say in private, but only after the election."

"You take your job very seriously, Lissa, Chuck told me, and that's great. Sometimes I feel disgusted with commentators, they distort what was said right in front of our eyes, they think we the public are stupid!"

"They are trying to push their personal views on the public and that is not honest journalism. I'm very careful with the words I use. Words are powerful!"

"They are, they can lead a crowd into greatness or madness."

"You are absolutely right, Douglas."

"Will you tell me all of your impressions after the election?"

"Yes, I will."

Douglas went outside to get his grandsons, Charles and Colin went to the stables. Grandma Tori was taking a nap in her chair, and I went to the kitchen to offer help to Magdalene and Kristin.

"No, just sit down, Lissa, or go upstairs to rest, you had a long trip and we have everything ready for tonight's dinner."

"I'm so impressed, you have prepared so much food. Did you do it all alone?"

"No, not really, I got help. And besides, cooking is a hobby for me."

"I want to learn all of Chuck's favorites, sometimes he tells me about the foods that you cook just for him and I have no idea how to prepare them."

"You'll learn, I'll show you."

Charles and Colin came back in. "Come, Lis, I want to show you the horses, maybe you would like to go for a horseback ride."

"Chuck, I never rode a horse!"

"I forgot, City Girl, I'll teach you tomorrow."

Kristin and Colin's sons Josh and Ryan came in, and she

introduced me as Aunt Lissa.

We all sat for dinner.

"It's just a family dinner tonight, tomorrow we will have Grandma's birthday celebration," Magdalene told us.

Grandma Tori spoke to me in front of everyone:

"When Chuck told us you were Gypsy I thought I was going to meet a voluptuous brunette, that is when he said you look like me. What is it like being Gypsy?"

The others got a little uncomfortable with her remark. I didn't.

"I don't know, I was never a good Gypsy girl, I was the odd one, and you are right... When I was fourteen my mother had my hair colored black and took me to a tanning salon to look more attractive, still I didn't fit in."

They laughed and I continued, "What I wanted to do with my life was not part of my family's plan, but if my grandmother were alive, I'm sure she would have supported me, she was lively like you. You remind me of her, Grandma Tori."

Grandma Tori brought me back memories of my own Grandma, my Bunica. She had a lot to live, if she could see me now...

After dinner, while serving desert, unexpectedly Charles spoke:

"I don't want to take the attention away from Grandma Tori's big day, but on this occasion I want to share with my family that Lissa and I have discussed our future. Let's make it official: Will you marry me, Lis?"

"Chuck! Oh, Chuck! Yes, I will marry you."

There were many hugs and kisses and welcomes to the family. Magdalene brought us champagne to celebrate. All of a sudden I became part of the family, a group of people that hardly knew me but love and respect their son's choices. It was the most amazing feeling, I belonged with Charles and his family.

Grandma Tori asked, "Where is the ring, Chuck?"

"Grandma, I'll be giving Lissa an engagement ring when we go back to DC, this is your party!"

"May your wedding be here and soon, I don't know how long I'm going to be around, I'm ninety..."

"Grandma, you are going to be at our wedding, I promise."

We stayed up until late, but before Grandma went to bed she asked me, "Do you wake up early, Lissa?"

"Usually I do."

"I want to talk to you in the morning, I am going to show you around."

"Alright, Grandma Tori, see you in the morning."

That evening in bed with Charles, I hugged him.

"Thank you for the surprise announcement, and I love being here with you and your family, they make me feel that I belong."

"You do belong, Lis, right here with me, you are part of the family now and thank you for going along with the plans to wed here. It means so much to them."

"Means much to me, Chuck, I missed not having a family, and now that I have one, I will nurture it. Besides I can see that you being here makes them happy. Did you see your Mom's expression? She was teary."

"I know. And Grandma Tori, did you see her excitement? She liked you at first sight. I also told Colin about my announcement when we went to the stables earlier, I did not want to leave him out."

"I am glad you included them all, this is an important day for us, for all of us."

I was up early the next morning and left Charles still sleeping. Grandma Tori was ready downstairs, waiting for me. She served me breakfast first.

"Happy Birthday, Grandma Tori! Great day to celebrate."

"Thank you, my dear, I can't believe I came this far. I am the oldest person that lived in this family, all the ones before me left much earlier..."

"You look fantastic and you have a great disposition, that will keep you going for a long time, Grandma."

"Come with me, Lissa, I want to show you a special place."

As we were leaving, Magdalene came downstairs. "Where are you going? Today is your birthday, Mom Tori, please stay in, you can talk to Lissa right here."

"First I am going to show her something. Let's go, Lissa."

We went to the garage where she had her vehicle, a golf cart.

"Doug gave me this one years ago, he prohibited me from riding horses or driving the Jeep. This little thing is slow but takes us around."

"It's cute! And I like to see the grounds. Yesterday when we came in, I was surprised by the beauty and the enormity of the land."

"Lissa, now that you are coming into our family I feel like I want to tell you my and my Albert's love story!"

"Oh, the other Albert and Victoria love story! Like Queen Victoria and her Prince!"

While she drove the cart through pathways and dirt roads, I felt like I was in a magical world. Everything around me looked astoundingly beautiful, the bluest sky, the purest breeze, but I paid close attention to her words.

"Behind that hill by the trees is my favorite place, my memory garden, for me it is the Garden of Eden."

"Eden? That was my Grandma's name, I know it is a biblical term that means the Garden of God. Mystical!"

"That's where my Albert and all my loved ones are, that is where I'll be with them soon...

I met Albert when I was a teenager. I lived in Des Moines and he was a student at the Agriculture School. He was five years older than me, and friends with one of my cousins, he came to a family party and that is how we met. He asked me to dance and in that first moment we fell in love...

It was magical, my first and only love. My parents didn't want us to get serious, but we couldn't help it.

When we graduated, me from high school and him from college, we got married and that's when I came to the farm, this magnificent land, seventy two years ago! A lifetime.

I was very happy with Albert during all the years of our marriage. We were so close, not even the biggest challenges could break us apart, we found solace in each other, and I love him until this day and can't wait to be reunited with him again. Here we are!"

She stopped by a lot surrounded by trees, a graveyard covered by beds of flowers with simple stones marking the graves. She walked to an iron bench under a shady tree, I followed her.

"Sit with me, Lissa. Here they are, my loved ones."

I saw Albert Hartsplend's grave, and right next to it another name: Charles Albert, 1942-1967.

"Charles?" I exclaimed.

"Charles was my firstborn son."

"I'm shocked, I'm so sorry, Grandma Tori. Chuck never told me about his Uncle Charles. He died so young!"

"My Charles was a dreamer, he wanted to fly high, during his years in high school he started taking flying lessons in Iowa City. He was planning to buy a one engine airplane to travel around this area, and Albert decided to build a runway on the property. We didn't oppose his dreams.

We were a very happy family until Charles, like his father, went to Agriculture School, but by the end of the first year he put it on hold and told us that he was joining the Air Force.

Albert and I were devastated, we were afraid he could eventually be deployed to the war in Vietnam, and that is exactly what happened.

At the Air Force base, he was trained on the F-105 Bombers and sent to a bombing campaign in North Vietnam in 1967, when they decimated that area with tons of missiles and bombs. During one of those operations my son's plane was brought down.

We found out days later that Charles was gone in that atrocious war, and they could not locate his body... For us he was not a body, he was our beloved son!"

Tears were rolling down Grandma Tori's face and mine. I held her, "I'm so sorry, Grandma Tori."

She cried for a while, the pain of losing her son was still vivid.

"He was never found, symbolically we brought him home and we made this memorial in this beautiful garden where I could always come to visit and pay homage to him. I was so proud of my son, he was fearless!

After we lost Charles, Albert was never the same, the light was gone out of his eyes, he slowed down. When Doug returned from school he started taking his father's responsibilities. A couple of years after Doug was married, Albert left us too and he never met

79

our grandson Charles, who, by the way, looks a lot like our lost son.

I needed to visit them today. I can't believe I got to be this age without them... Thank you for listening to me, Lissa."

"Thank you for sharing your poignant life story with me, Grandma Tori. I am sure they are both very proud of you in Heaven."

"Now you can better understand why I was so upset when my grandson Charles left for the military. It was painful, but thank God he survived the war, he is back and well and happy with you now, but Magda, Doug and I still dream of him coming back home. Do you think that could happen?"

"I don't know, Grandma Tori. Chuck tells me that he loves his family and this land, but he just felt the call of duty and a passion for national security."

"Lissa, would you support him if he decides to return home?"

"I would, I think he needs to be where his heart is, I would support him if that is what he wants to do."

"Thank you, Lissa. Do you want to try to drive this thing back? I am a little tired now."

"Sure, it will be fun, please show me the way."

We arrived back at the house, and everybody was a little rushed because we took too long.

Magdalene told Grandma to get ready, "Your guests are going to start showing up."

Charles told me that the farm workers were coming by the house to wish her a happy birthday. "Grandma is loved by all!"

"I can see why."

At noon Magdalene, Kristin and the boys set up tables to put food and beverages out on the front porch for the workers, managers of the leased parcels and their families.

Grandma, all dressed up, sat, and people started coming with flowers, many flowers. She was smiling.

By midafternoon she went inside, "I had too much fun for today, I am going to take a nap now."

Charles took me out on a horse. I was scared, but I survived. We stepped away from the others.

"You don't have to tell me where Grandma took you earlier... To the Garden of Eden, I bet."

"Yes, and I was very touched, also very surprised by the revelation. You never mention your Uncle Charles, I know you didn't meet him... but..."

"That's a very painful chapter in my family's life. And sincerely now that I am older I can appreciate how much I made them suffer when I went away... For them it was like Vietnam all over again."

"Chuck, you know they still pray for you to come home, don't you?"

"I am not ready to make that decision, but it does cross my mind... What do you think, Lis? Would you support me?"

"Grandma asked me the same question and I said yes, you need to be where your heart is."

He hugged me and we kissed.

"You are so right for me and my family, Lis, my love."

That evening we celebrated Grandma's birthday in style, some people came from town, old friends and their pastor. Grandma discussed our wedding with him.

After a few more days together, and some horseback rides, many conversations with the family, incredible sights, breathing the purest air under the most clear starry sky, we bonded. "I'll miss them all."

We said our goodbyes, I was emotional. I told Grandma Tori that being around her, I felt like I had my own grandmother back in my life.

That was for me also a good occasion to know Colin and Kristin. He was polite, but a little cold. Kristin was very bubbly and warm. She told me:

"I am from this area, I went to Des Moines for college, then I moved to the farm when I married Colin, but I still go to town every day, I am a teacher at the high school. We, the town residents, love to have new people around, and I personally would love for you to come often, Lissa."

"Thank you, Kristin, I feel very welcomed and I will come back here as much as I can. And I appreciate knowing you're a teacher, it is a noble profession!"

I was also impressed by Doug's nurturing interaction with his super active grandsons. "Where do they get all that energy from?"

He told me he wished he had more time to spend with the boys. "I don't want to force them into being farmers, I want them to have the best childhood possible and offer them guidance to make their future choices. But deep inside I hope they'll keep working on this land, Ryan and Josh are our future!"

On the way back to the airport I learned more about Cedar Rapids, the city on the banks of the river with the same name.

"It's the second largest city in Iowa!"

"That view of the new buildings by the river and the bridges impresses me. I like it, Chuck."

"Cedar Rapids is also the center of arts and culture of eastern Iowa, with museums, a library, theater, orchestra... Everything you would wish for entertainment."

"Next time I'll make time to visit the library, it is my old tradition, I visit libraries everywhere I go. Do your parents come here often, Chuck?"

"They do, mostly Dad, he comes for his meetings at the Soybean Farmers Association, he is the president. They also come to the theater sometimes."

"It's a nice place to live! I only knew Iowa City, when I came to cover a caucus. What about Des Moines? How far is it from here?"

"About one hundred miles, it's accessible, the largest city in the state, with more to do and see."

"Thank you, Chuck, for bringing me here to join your family, our family. I'm so touched by this experience. I came to Iowa to celebrate Grandma's birthday and we return engaged, making plans for our wedding, for a life together."

One of the first things we did in DC when we returned... Charles took me to a fancy jewelry store in Chevy Chase and got me the most beautiful, classy diamond ring. A solitaire!

We celebrated our engagement, just the two of us, with much love.

I should be feeling so happy! My heart was full of love and new emotions, but I was torn inside, anguished and distressed, my mind was filled with buried, confusing images that were coming to the surface as nightmares and flashbacks.

"She hoped to be wise and reasonable in time..."[16]

I needed to do something about it!

CHAPTER FIVE

MY SOUL

*D*ays later I went to see my therapist.

"This seems unreal, am I losing my mind?" I knew I appeared bewildered.

Dr. Aldrin asked me, "Can you identify those memories and feelings?"

"I can, but it is all terrifying, no matter what, I am committed to restoring myself. I longed to learn how I should handle these feelings. Please, I am counting on your guidance and support."

"Lissa, when we start digging in, it usually gets worse before it gets better, but you will overcome your memories, they won't overpower you, we can work through this."

I learned that hidden stress in consequence of trauma as a child may cause health issues later on. That was a price I was not willing to pay, I wanted my life to be in balance and I started the most arduous part of my treatment, coming to grips with frightening images trapped in my brain for so long, believing that I had the power to heal myself.

As weeks went by I couldn't plan my future until I had the clarity to overcome past torments. I made an effort to keep this emotional turmoil from Charles, I didn't want to spoil our time together, a time of love, closeness.

Our professional lives got busy, and Charles went on another trip abroad.

As the tensions of my work preceding the political campaign started getting overwhelming that soon in the game, so did my mood. I became irritable and showed very little patience.

Deborah asked me what was going on with me. "You seem overwhelmed, Lissa."

"I am afraid of losing control, I am having a hard time dealing with everything, and the constant chatter in the news is tiring me. Oh, my soul yearns for peace!"

"Take a break, Lissa, follow your own path and take time to write your story. Putting things in writing it becomes clear, and through it you'll find healing and maybe bring hope to others in similar situations."

Deborah is an emotionally intelligent person and she is right, writing is healing, and I will do that one day after this is all resolved. I am restless now, but I will follow my own path...

Summer was going by fast...

Charles and I had the chance to spend a long weekend with Kevin, Suzy and their children in North Carolina. I truly enjoyed our friends' company. I needed that mental and physical break.

With Suzy we only talked about trivial things, and that was refreshing for all of us.

Charles and I had an amazing, loving time talking about our upcoming wedding, our future plans... We are connected in a way that I never thought possible, he deserves the best of me!

Magdalene called us several times with suggestions for our wedding. I couldn't decide anything about the preparations, I left it all up to her. I didn't tell her what I was dealing with and made excuses about my busy work schedule.

Before the summer's end Charles also asked me to confirm the date.

"My folks suggested that we have the wedding by the Fall Festival in October. Do you think it will be possible, Lis?"

"I have been overwhelmed, Chuck, I need a little more time, please."

"Lis, I am concerned you are having night terrors, crying in your sleep. Is Dr. Aldrin helping you? What is going on?"

"Dr. Aldrin told me that when we are in an intimate relationship, most of the time the issues from our primary relationships in childhood surface and we feel lost. Chuck, this is all about an old issue and it will never go away if I don't face it. I am determined to resolve it, I promise you and myself."

"Darling, this is related to your father, isn't it?"

"It is. I was just a little girl, I couldn't do anything, I feel so guilty…"

I broke into tears, Charles held me.

"I understand, darling, I'll help you any way I can. Are you ready to tell me about it?"

I sobbed uncontrollably.

"Please give me a little more time, first I need to clear my mind, make a plan and then get the courage to release this torment from my heart. Then I'll be free to marry you, to be your wife and be able to create happiness for us!"

"I am with you all the way! Remember, darling, you are not alone, you have my full support."

At my office, dealing with an intern reporter, I became very frustrated.

"Look how you use your words, making a statement that a candidate made 'false accusations' about a fact that was not investigated or confirmed yet is wrong! You need to say 'unsubstantiated' or 'unproven facts' until it is actually confirmed that it's false or not. Beware of your words! Don't try to influence the public's opinion. Always be truthful!"

The young man was startled. I felt horrible, I overreacted!

"I'm sorry if I was too strong on you. That's the principle I live and work by, the truth! Nothing but the truth…"

The young man left and I stood up in front of the framed Journalist's Creed posted on my office wall, and in that moment I understood why I was so ambivalent about my personal issues.

Some phrases from the Creed always stand out to me:

'I believe that a journalist should write only what he holds in his heart to be true.'

'That a single standard of helpful truth and cleanness should prevail for all…'

'I believe that suppression of the news, for any consideration other than the welfare of society, is indefensible.'

From that moment on, I started feeling more relaxed, and when Charles came back from another assignment, I was ready to talk to him.

"I'm so glad you are back, my love, I missed you so."

"You look calmer, Lis. Is everything alright now? Are you anticipating to take time off for our wedding?"

"Before that, I have to do something very demanding, I'll tell you later, Chuck. Come, you need to eat and rest first."

After dinner I took him to our bedroom.

"No TV tonight, I'm ready to talk to you. Everything became crystal clear, I was able to remember all the details with clarity and I made a plan of action to execute as soon as possible."

"I am all ears, darling."

I finally spoke, told Charles everything...

"This is the most difficult action I would ever have to take in my life, but if I don't, I will never let go of this devastating burden from my heart."

He agreed with me, he held me. I cried in his arms, releasing years of anguish. Finally, after twenty five years of carrying a secret, I was ready to face it.

"I was only a child, I was so afraid, couldn't do anything! My little girl brain buried and denied the painful events, and that's how I grew up, not really understanding why I was hated and mistreated by my own father. I felt lost about myself and an enormous sense of guilt took over me. But then came you, your love lifted me up and I started feeling and seeing things clearly."

"No, darling, you couldn't do anything then, I can't imagine how much this has weighed on your soul. I admire that you had the strength to break away and live your life the way you did."

"I have to go back there, Chuck, I need to face evil to be able to let go..."

"I agree, I'll come with you, darling."

"It's not that I want to leave you out, I have to do this on my own. I am embarrassed about bringing you into that hateful environment. Please understand, I need to face them by myself."

"Alright, Lis, but I won't let you go alone, I want you to be protected."

"I'm so exhausted now."

I fell asleep in Charles' arms, feeling comforted and light.

With the help of a private investigator, plus my own research, days later I got an update on the Thoor family in West Virginia. Sadly I found out that my brother Darien had been killed in a fight shortly after I ran away, he was only nineteen years old. I was devastated.

I tried to come to terms with it, went back in my old memories just to realize that, although living under the same roof with my siblings, we hardly had anything in common.

We were divided in my household, boys were raised one way and girls another. Family unity was not promoted among us, which absolutely did not depend on us children.

I felt deeply sad, I had a brother that was only two years older than me that I hardly had any memory of. I remembered him as a little boy. Would he have turned out to be like Father?

I also found out that Melinda was married at age eighteen and divorced at twenty one, and confirmed that my parents still live in the same house, close to Ingleside.

I made a few phone calls to Princeton for the necessary arrangements, then discussed with Charles that I was ready to go next week and I needed to spend two days there.

"I am in the middle of a very serious project, but I can't let you go alone, I'm calling Ruben, he has a security company, he will drive you and will stay with you at all times."

"Alright, Chuck, I understand you are trying to protect me, but who is Ruben? A bodyguard?"

"You haven't met him yet. He was also a Marine and now he is a high level security guard. He is a big guy, very strong and impressive, but he is reliable and caring. I trust him to keep you safe."

Charles called Ruben, and he came to meet me in my office the next day.

I liked him, he spoke softly to me and had an impressive presence.

"I'll drive you and I'll stay with you."

"We will have to stay overnight, I'm making reservations at the Holiday Inn. As a matter of fact I like that you are coming with me, Ruben, it is a five hour drive from DC to Princeton, and on the way I will tell you what I am going for, you should know what to expect."

We left at daybreak on Tuesday. During the long drive Ruben gave me some advice on how to approach my family.

"Be calm, say everything you need to say, don't show any vacillation and everything will be alright! I will be by your side."

"Thank you, Ruben. I pray to be fair and in control of my emotions!"

*"Pray, pray be composed... and do not betray what you feel to everybody present."*17

He spent a long time talking about his family, his children, about how he was brought up in Alabama by his devoted Mama to be the man he is. He also spoke of his admiration for Charles.

"I was one of the guys that he saved on one of our missions, I owe him my life."

"I didn't know that, Chuck never told me."

"That's why I committed to this job, usually I do not travel this far, but I'll do anything for my friend, and here I am to protect you, Lissa."

"Thank you so much, Ruben, I feel good in your presence, count me as your friend too."

We arrived in Princeton around 11:30 a.m.

"Would you like to have lunch now, Ruben?"

"I just want to stretch my legs and get coffee, then we'll proceed to your family's house."

"It's only four miles from here. I'm getting so nervous being back after seventeen years... My heart is racing! I dread going there."

"I understand, rely on me, you are not alone."

"One does not love a place the less for having suffered in it, unless it has been all suffering, nothing but suffering..."[18]

He drove to the house, parked the SUV and walked with me to the front door. I was composed, apparently very calm. I rang the bell.

A young woman opened the door and stared at me. "Why did you park in my driveway? What do you want?"

Oh, I knew that face!

"Melinda, Melie, it's me, your sister Monalissa."

"Mona? Mona, you are back!" She shouted, "Mom, come and see who's here!"

Mother came and didn't smile, just stood there, visibly surprised to see me.

"How are you, Mother? This is my friend Ruben. Are you going to invite us in?"

"What are you doing here, Mona?"

"I want to talk to you and Rufus."

She let us in. Melie offered us a seat.

The house looked clean as always, but run-down. Some of the old pieces of furniture were the same, nothing much changed from the time I left... But my mother had lost her youthful glow, she looked old and sad.

She spoke first, "Your father is sick, you can't see him. What do you want to talk to us about? Are you here for revenge?"

"No, I am here for justice! Please call him."

"He doesn't want to talk to you."

Melie stepped in, "Mom, let's get over this, I'll call Dad." She walked to the bedroom.

Ruben was sitting across from us in the living room, observing us.

"Mona, what are you doing with your life? Where do you live?" Mother asked me.

"First, no one calls me Mona, I am Lissa. I am a journalist and I live in Washington, DC. Mother, I heard of Darien's death and I am very sorry you lost your son."

She showed no emotion.

"It was a silly fight over a girl, he was so young, it is all in the past now…"

"What about Dylan and Miranda? Are they alright?"

"Dylan lives close by, he is in charge of Father's business. Mira is a rich woman, she still lives in Martinsburg, I don't see her often."

Melinda came back, "Sorry, I insisted, Dad doesn't want to see you, he is not coming here… He is sick."

"In that case, Mother, let's go to his room. I won't leave without talking to him."

"Leave your friend here, you should come alone."

"No, Ruben will come, he can stay outside the door, my fiancé asked him to be with me at all times."

"Who is he? Your bodyguard? Why do you need one?"

We walked into the hallway to the master bedroom. My mother opened the door, and I saw a weak, skinny old man reclining on the bed. For a moment I felt compassion for him. The muscular, strong man was gone, but not his harsh and loud voice…

"I said I don't want to see you or hear from you, get out of my house!"

I didn't feel intimidated at all, "I see you are sick, but still able to yell. Yes, Rufus, whether you like it or not, we are going to talk today."

"What do you want? Did you come here to torture me? What's that guy doing here? I don't invite that kind of people into my house."

I had a sinking feeling, turned around and apologized to Ruben.

"Rufus, you haven't changed at all, old, sick, but still the same angry, ignorant man. Ruben stays, he is my friend, we will both leave your house when I am done. Let's make this quick and easy.

I came here today to offer you an opportunity of redemption, of making amends, to free yourself from guilt or remorse, if you have any, for what you have done, and in the process I am releasing the little girl that has carried this pain and this burden for twenty five years... Oh, you can't possibly understand what you did to me, there were two victims... And finally I am here for justice!"

"You are a traitor, a coward, you have no respect for an old, sick man, I can't leave this bed, I don't have much time to live..."

I responded loud and clear..."You are right, I lost respect for you long ago, and you know very well what a coward is, that's what you always have been, Rufus. I didn't know I was going to find you sick, but I still have compassion for you, for your soul, I am offering you an opportunity. You are saying you won't live long, you might be right. In that case how do you want to meet your Creator? You do believe in heaven and hell, you were a churchgoer as far as I remember. This is your opportunity to repent, to free yourself from your crime."

"You are crazy, you're a blabber mouth, stupid girl. I have nothing to repent, nothing. Get out of my house!" he yelled with all his lungs.

"No, Rufus, I am not a stupid girl, not eight years old anymore. For far too long I carried this horrible feeling of guilt about the past, as if I could have done anything, I had a void in my heart, a dark hole, carrying your secret, not mine, yours, that is coming out today!

Let's make this short, too much time has gone by and I have a question for you: Why? Why did you kill my Grandma? Was it out of anger or because you were drunk that night? Or was it for her house and money? Why did you kill her? I demand you answer me!"

He yelled as loud as he could:

"Shut up! Get out! Angelika, take her out of here."

Mother gasped, "Mona, don't accuse your father, you should be loyal to him, to us. Did you come to destroy our lives?"

"Loyal? Like you, Mother? You concealed his crime, you are his loyal accomplice, don't put me in the same category. I am loyal to my Grandma, your mother, and I want justice for her. That's where my loyalty rests, with truth and justice."

Rufus sat on the bed, propelled by his anger, shouting:

"I should have killed you too, like I did her! You are just like her, you think you are better than me..."

"I have no doubt you could have killed me, you were strong like an enraged bull. You can't deny it, Rufus, you know I saw you suffocating Bunica with a pillow. You left the door open, there was some light coming in from the hallway, I thought you came to give her the inhaler, but you covered her face with the pillow and kept pushing it down, she kicked for a little while.

I thought I was having a bad dream, I called you, 'What are you doing, Dad?'

You were obviously startled, you didn't expect me to be here. You came to me, punched my head so strongly, everything blacked out.

I woke up to a lot of commotion in this same room, you were here too, Mother. I had a bump on my right temple, my head was pounding. I called Bunica. You, Rufus, grabbed me by my arm and threw me outside the room. I hit the wall and stayed there, unable to move, shaking and crying.

You threatened to kill me if I said a word. I knew you would have."

Mother started crying, "Stop, Mona, please stop, it was so long ago, you got what you came for, now please leave, please."

"Mother, you are an accomplice, you knew, and when I told you what I saw, you slapped me on the face, adding more injury to the ones he already had inflicted on me, and told me never to repeat that again.

Were you in on it too? Was it planned? Did you want her house and her money for yourself?

She was your mother, a wonderful woman that gave you everything. He took her life, your husband murdered your mother and you stood by him and still want to protect him? Not anymore, you'll have to respond to the authorities too…"

I looked over my shoulder, Ruben was standing still, very stern. At his side Melinda was crying, my heart broke for her.

"Rufus, I am offering you the opportunity to come clean and maybe you'll get a deal with law enforcement. I wrote an affidavit, a fair confession from you explaining what happened. Mother can read it to you, and you should sign it. Let's make this easy."

"I'll never confess and no one will ever believe you, you are revengeful. If I had finished you then, you would not be accusing me now."

"Are you sure, Rufus? You already confessed. Did you hear everything, Ruben? Melinda also heard you."

I showed him my iPad.

"And I have it all recorded, yes, the Prosecutor will believe me. I have an appointment with him in one hour. You are going to face the law, you have no choice, Rufus. It gives me some relief to tell you to your face: You are a murderer! You are my Grandma's killer and you are going to pay for it.

The truth is out today! There is no way out for you."

There was a jar with water by his side table, he grabbed it and threw it at me. Ruben pushed me away quickly, the jar exploded against the wall, spreading shards of glass all over. Ruben pulled me to the side and put up his hands towards Rufus, "Easy, man, easy! I won't let you hurt her! Calm down!"

Melinda ran to the living room.

I looked around, stared at Rufus one last time.

"This is where you killed her, your bed is in the same position hers was. How were you able to rest or sleep in this room for all these years?

You took my Grandma's life, you hurt me badly, but you did not break my spirit. You didn't count on that, did you, Rufus? You are a monster, a murderer!"

I spoke firmly in total control of my emotions, I didn't cry and I meant every word I said. I didn't need to say anything else, and that gave me the deepest relief I ever felt. I turned to Ruben, "I have nothing else to do here."

Mother followed us, begging me, "You got him to admit it, please don't get the police involved. He is very sick, his liver is destroyed by cirrhosis, let him go in peace..."

"In peace? My Grandma didn't die in peace, I didn't live in peace until now... Did you? Do you have a conscience? You are heartless! I'm done with you, but before I go, take this."

I gave her an envelope containing cash.

"This is the money, with interest, that you gave me when I

escaped. I don't owe you anything. Anything!"

I turned to Melinda, she was crying.

"Sorry, Melie, I didn't want to cause you any distress. You'll be alright, you have nothing to do with this mess, you were not even born when it happened."

"But I suspected it, Mona, sometimes when he was drunk, he bragged, 'It was easy to kill the old witch just with a pillow…'"

"In that case I have one more witness, you, Melie. Thank you for telling me."

"I want to talk to you before you leave for DC, can I see you later?"

"Yes, tomorrow, but I won't return to this house. Where should we meet, Melie?"

"I work at the bridal store, Sonja's, remember? Can you stop by? I'll be there all day."

"Do you work with Sonja? Absolutely, I'll see you there. Stay calm."

Ruben and I went to the Prosecutor's Office for our appointment.

"I'm sorry to get you involved with this, Ruben, you are going to be asked to tell what you've witnessed and heard."

"When it comes to putting a murderer behind bars, I have no problem. What a coward, killing an old lady and trying to kill his own child. You did incredibly well, you should be proud of yourself."

"Till this moment I never knew myself." *[19]

We stayed at the Prosecutor's Office until 7:00 p.m. He heard my story, I signed my deposition. They did the same with Ruben and they scheduled a meeting first thing the next morning with the Police Chief.

Ruben and I were exhausted, physically and emotionally. We went for a good dinner and did not speak about the eventful day.

We took our rooms at the hotel.

I called Charles.

"It's all over, a ton of weight has been lifted from my heart. I'm so glad you sent Ruben with me, he protected me and in the end he became a witness."

"I'm relieved, darling, I thought of you and what you are going through all day, it almost stopped me from doing my work. I can't wait to have you back home, Lis."

"I'll be home tomorrow, free to start our new life together. I'm free, Chuck!"

We met at the Prosecutor's Office with the Police Chief in the morning, a warrant for Rufus and Angelika's arrest was made.

The Prosecutor told me that, depending on their plea, they could make a deal and a trial wouldn't be necessary. But no matter what, Rufus was going to prison. I had offered enough evidence.

"What about my mother? What is going to happen to her?"

"I don't know yet, it all depends on her deposition, we are treating her as an accomplice at this point."

"Please be soft on my little sister, she was not even born when that all happened, she is an innocent bystander."

The Prosecutor and the Police Chief both told me they would be in contact with me throughout the process, and in the case of a trial I would need to come back to depose.

"I'll collaborate, but sincerely I hope this is the end of this story for me."

Ruben went to a coffee shop while I went to Sonja's Bridal. I saw Sonja, now an old lady, "Your sister told me you were coming today, you are the bride that ran away…"

"Yes, Sonja, so long ago. I never thought I would come back to your store… I'm surprised that Melie works here with you."

"She is great with the customers and she is talented, she designs too!"

Melinda came out of the dressing room.

Sonja gave her some time off to talk to me. We went to a coffee shop next door.

"I want to talk about you, but before that, I need to tell you that today Rufus and Mother are being arrested. The Police Chief and the Prosecutor are going to call you to depose, don't be afraid or intimidated, I told them you have nothing to do with this issue, and again I'm sorry for the way things came out, I waited too long, Melie, I couldn't remain silent anymore."

"I know, I can't imagine what you went through, now I totally understand why you ran away. I missed you so much after you left, I prayed for you to come back, you finally did."

"Oh, my little sister, I'm so sorry. What did they tell you after I left? How did they treat you? Was he aggressive with you too?"

"Mom told me you had gone to school far away and I shouldn't ask about you again... Father was mad, cursing and yelling, and he forbade everyone from mentioning you. He was not aggressive with me, but was not caring either. I was just there, I never got close to him."

"I dreaded to think he could hurt you, I lost sleep over it... What about Mother? Was she loving to you?"

"I became her only daughter and she started taking me to all of her activities and parties, weddings, baptisms, birthdays... I think that was her way of being a loving mother. But I missed you, no matter what, I never forgot you."

"Melie, I found out you are divorced. Do you have any children?"

Melinda's eyes welled up.

"I have a little boy, four years old. He is with his father. He got custody."

"Why? Do you see your son?"

"I do sometimes. He lives in Bluefield. The law is not fair to women, I lost my boy because I was the one asking for the divorce, I didn't love Tim Ray anymore, it was horrible being married to him, but I have to be fair, he is a good father. Timmy, my boy, is happy."

"Did Rufus force you to marry Tim?"

"No, it was my choice, the wrong choice, I got pregnant and..."

"Are you a designer? How did Mother allow you to work outside the home? That was against her rules!"

"I always loved to draw, I never went to school, I wish I could become a fashion designer, a real one.

Mother allowed me to work because they need the money,

97

that's the only reason. I have to pay to live in their house.

Sometimes I just want to go away from here, but I can't go far, I have my son..."

"Melie, I am going to give you my phone numbers, if you need any help please contact me. I am so sorry I left you, I have thought of you all of these years, I will always be your big sister."

"I'm glad you are back in my life, Mona."

"I changed my name, I'm Lissa. That's how Grandma Eden used to call me. One thing before I go… Do you know the directions to the family grave? I want to stop by on my way out of town."

"Mom didn't talk much about our grandmother. Would you tell me about her next time I see you?"

"Sure, Melie, I'd love to."

We hugged, we promised to stay in touch.

Melinda gave me directions. I left with my heart hurting for her.

Ruben stopped at the cemetery. The grave was totally abandoned, looked like no one ever visits. Grandma's name was engraved on a headstone, and by her side, Darien's. So sad!

I talked to her, oh, if only she could hear me…

'Bunica, I finally brought you justice, I never forgot you and never will. I did everything you expected me to do… As an homage to you, I read all the books you appreciated and repeated your famous quotes and I still do every day.

Bunica, you are part of me, and no matter how short our life together was, you made the biggest impact.

I was and I am proud of being your granddaughter. I will always love you. Be in peace.'

I cried almost all the way back to DC. I told Ruben:

"As an eight year old girl I blamed myself for my Grandma's death, I thought if I had only found her inhaler she would be alive… The horrific memory of her death was buried in me until it started flashing back… It was like torture, it ripped my heart apart, but now I am free! I am finally free!"

He tried to cheer me up, "You are letting go of hurt feelings,

98

anxieties of all these years, it was too much for a little girl to carry. You did right for you and your grandmother. You brought her peace!"

We have a remarkable bond, Ruben and I. The bond of justice.

We arrived home in DC very late. I hugged him.
"Thank you, brother, for being with me on this journey."

Charles was anxiously waiting. He took me in his arms.
"I'll never let you go, if you need to go back to West Virginia I'll come with you."
"I hope it won't be necessary to go back, it was emotionally charged, I am exhausted. From now on, it is only about our lives and our future."

Charles held me all night, and I felt loved, protected.

In the morning, feeling rested, I told him, "It is hard to believe that you loved me just the way I was, broken. The deepest feelings I developed for you were the catalyst that propelled me out of the agony, our love brought me light, I was inspired and moved to be whole again and offer you the best of me. Chuck, you reached my soul and rescued me from a dark place."

"You pierce my soul. I am half agony, half hope... I have loved none but you." [20]

"Entering that house, walking into that hallway to the bedroom, for a moment I saw myself as a battered little girl crawled up against the wall, and when I saw Rufus old and frail, I felt compassion for a second and hoped that he would have turned out to be more human and show some remorse. The opposite happened, which gave me more courage to go on. I felt powerful.

When I was leaving, I looked at that corner, the memory of that little girl was not there anymore. It was cathartic!

Then when I visited the cemetery on my way out of town to say goodbye to my beloved Grandma, Bunica, I felt like she was in peace and I was healed."

"Lis, when I fell in love with you, I saw you as you are, a

strong, loving and capable woman. No one like you had crossed my path before. I knew it was you, the one I wanted to join my life with. I am glad that I have a part in resolving this chapter of your life. I am with you for better or worse, for always."

"Now it is our time to be happy!"

CHAPTER SIX

HAPPIEST

Charles reminded me that his parents were anxiously waiting to confirm our wedding at the Fall Festival that was coming up.

"Don't you think it is too soon, Chuck? I had no time to prepare anything. Would they mind if we do it by Thanksgiving?"

"It looks like they are in a hurry for us to get married, I personally think that Thanksgiving is better. This is a very busy time at the farm, racing against the elements to get their crops in before the first frost and snowflakes fly, but you are going to miss the fields turning gold under the warm sunlight of the fall…"

"I'd like to see it, but I am sure we will have many other opportunities. To the farm we go in November, I'm ready to be Mrs. Charles Hartsplend!"

We called Magdalene, she was thrilled.

"Thanksgiving will be perfect! I'm so glad you are going along with our suggestion. It means so much to us, especially to Grandma Tori, she can't wait to see Chuck married here."

Melinda texted me saying that Mother and Father were arrested, but Mother returned home in two days, she made a deal with the Prosecutor. She told the truth about Rufus' actions, who was still claiming he was set up.

In another text she said our brother Dylan was mad at me for bringing this matter to the authorities. He will never forgive me.

It didn't faze me at all, "He better get over it!"

I called the Prosecutor's Office for an update. They informed me that to avoid jail time Mother disclosed all the facts, claiming battered wife syndrome, saying that Rufus was controlling and manipulative, and keeping things quiet was her only way of having some peace in the house.

According to her deposition, when the crime occurred, Rufus panicked and told her that he only took her mother 'out of her misery,' she was hardly breathing. My mother called the neighborhood family doctor that assisted Grandma and he believed that cardiac arrest was the cause of death. They were sure that no one would ever know.

Mother also confirmed to the Prosecutor that she knew I was a witness and that I had told the truth about what happened.

Not surprising to me, she always knew the truth, but I still wonder why she had hard feelings towards her own mother to the extreme of covering up for her murder... I'll never understand her.

Deborah called, asking me to come for a business meeting in her office.

"Lissa, I have an offer for you. I want you to co-chair my show and produce and present one segment, but you would have to leave your current position. I'm making you a very appealing financial offer."

She gave me a memo.

"Deborah, this is amazing!"

"Plus a two year contract, and in the event that I leave the news hour, the first chair will be yours! Another good payoff is that you won't be travelling much during the campaigns anymore, probably only to assist in the caucuses and conventions."

"That's fantastic! Thank you, Deb! When would you like me to start?"

"In January! So are you saying yes?"

"Yes, this is a great opportunity. Thank you for thinking of me. This job will suit my life perfectly. Charles and I set the date, we are getting married next month! Sorry, I would love to invite you, but it is going to be up on the farm in Iowa with his family."

"Congratulations, it's great! I am happy for both of you."

"Done deal, I'll call Chicago and send them my resignation. We are going to work really well together, I do appreciate your talent and work ethic, Deborah."

In the beginning of November Charles and Kevin went abroad, the last trip of the year. I sighed in relief, every time he is away I feel anxious. I went to see Suzy, I had told her about our upcoming wedding, she was excited for Charles and me.

"Suzy, it just occurred to me that I need a dress for my wedding... Would you like to help me find something suitable for a simple ceremony at the farm?"

"Definitely, I'd love to help you."

Shopping we went, and she made me buy a beautiful lace dress with long sleeves in a blush color that I thought was a little too fancy, I never wore anything so beautiful!

"Victorian style! It's perfect on you, Lissa, you'll look beautiful and regal on your wedding day!"

"Grandma Tori will appreciate it! And if my Grandma could see me now, I am sure she would love it too!"

That afternoon we returned to her house, we had tea together and I told my friend of last month's events in Princeton. Now I can talk easily with no shame of old secrets... She was shocked!

"And now you and everybody else knows everything about me, the dark past is gone and I am free to marry the man of my dreams. Suzy, I never thought it would be possible to feel this way."

I called my sister to tell her about my wedding.

"I want you to know that I am on my way to Iowa to get married at Charles' family farm. Sorry, Melie, it will be a very small ceremony and we are not inviting anyone. But when we are back I want you to come and see me here in DC. I would love to introduce you to Charles and spend time with you."

"I wish you all the happiness you deserve, Lissa, and I will come to see you. I love talking with you and I also would like to know more about our Grandmother Eden."

"I'll share all I know with you, Melie. Happy Thanksgiving!"

To Iowa we went, Charles and I talking about our present and making plans for our future. This is really a family affair.

These almost two years since we met have gone by fast, so much has happened, our feelings for one another deepened and grew, my life was totally transformed. I came out of my shell of emotional isolation, I was able to face the truth and the consequences, all because of the power of love and truth. With Charles, everything is possible, everything!

We both agreed in not telling his family about the last events in my family at this time.

"This is an occasion only to celebrate love and family and it is also a good time to talk about having a baby! What do you think, darling?"

"Oh, a baby! I am ready, Chuck, more than ready to start a family with you, my love."

Magdalene and Kristin had prepared a feast for us, I never saw anything like that. The farm looked completely different from the lush green fields in the spring, now covered in white snow glistening under the sunlight.

They invited the workers to be part of the festivity on our arrival the day before Thanksgiving.

"We are celebrating our son getting married here in our Splendland!"

Douglas thanked me, "It is wonderful of you to agree in marrying here, we have missed out on so much of our son's life since he moved away."

"I'm happy to be part of your family and we will come back often."

Grandma Tori hugged me. "I am your real Grandma now and I have a wedding present for you!"

She gave me an old, black velvet jewelry box, I opened it!

"Pearls! A pearl necklace!" I couldn't say anything else, tears started streaming down my face.

Grandma Tori continued, "I have given jewelry to both Magda and Kristin on their wedding days, they were gifts from my Albert to me. Now I am glad to offer you my favorite pearl necklace as I welcome you as my granddaughter."

Charles came closer and held me, "Don't worry, Grandma,

Lissa is very emotional these days!"

I finally was able to speak, I held her hand. "Grandma Tori, this means so much to me, more than you'll ever know. My Grandma Eden had a necklace just like this, one strand of pearls all the same size, so classy, she wore it all the time. Sometimes when the two of us had our tea parties, she would put her necklace on me, saying that it was going to be mine when I grew up… That day never came, after she was gone they pawned all of her jewelry, everything was lost… And now, here you are, giving me this precious necklace, oh, thank you, thank you, Grandma Tori."

"I understand, Lissa, you feel like your grandmother is here, blessing you on your wedding day. I am sure she is, things happened for a reason, I was guided to choose this piece for you, it is meant to be yours. In this case it is from both of your grandmothers with love."

I was so emotional, I thought I would never stop crying. I kissed my Grandma Tori.

Magdalene told us, "Dad and I want to give you a honeymoon at our favorite resort in Kohler, but when you said you couldn't stay for more than three days, we didn't make the reservations. If you want to go next spring or summer for a few days of rest and fun, tell us when you are ready for reservations. For now we have a surprise for both of you, Kristin and I prepared the guest house as your honeymoon suite, but you can only stay there tomorrow for your wedding night…"

"Thank you, Mom and Dad, this is so thoughtful, 'a honeymoon suite' just for us!"

Charles invited his brother to stand with him, and Kristin was my maid of honor. Colin was friendlier this time than when I first met him in May. He was emotional, hugging Charles and wishing us happiness.

Magdalene was smiling, her sons are on the right path to reconciling their differences…

The next day they brought their pastor and he performed a touching ceremony in the main house.

Charles and I were emotional. Everyone was!

"Chuck, I think I am in a dream, I am marrying the love of my life, it could not be more perfect today!"

"I have looked for you, Lis, I didn't know where you were, but unexpectedly I found you, I took you in my arms and *'My lonely days were over and life was like a song,'* our love song."

It's official, we are husband and wife.
We celebrated!

Grandma Tori couldn't stop complimenting my dress. "I love it so much, you couldn't look any more beautiful than this."

"Thank you, Grandma, I had you in mind, it is a Victorian style."

Later, Charles and I were alone in our lovely suite... "How do you feel, my wife?"

"Happier than I have ever been, my husband."

"Thank you for marrying me here, it means so much to my parents, we made them happy today. A Thanksgiving Day to remember!"

"It means much more to me to be part of your family, to be your wife, my love."

"How shall I bear so much happiness!"*21

After a couple of days of loving time, we left. I felt nostalgic saying goodbye, but with a heart full of joy, love and gratitude for this most meaningful celebration.

Charles and I could not come back in four weeks for the holidays this year, due to our work commitments.

We spent one more day in our apartment celebrating our marriage, and on Tuesday we both went back to work.

That same week I was informed by the Princeton Prosecutor's Office that Rufus took the plea for manslaughter, with a sentence of twenty years, and his justification was that he liked the free medical treatment he was getting in jail... The Prosecutor told me

106

he won't serve long... There is no cure for his condition, his health is deteriorating.

I felt a sense of relief, I'll never have to go back there, ever again. As my new happy life starts, my old life ended.

The only contact that I will maintain is with Melinda.

She told me that Mother is being ostracized from the community, her friends deserted her, horrified by the fact that she covered up her mother's murder.

"Gypsies are unforgiving."

"That is unforgivable in any culture, Melie!"

"Lissa, I'd like your advice about completing school... I am also moving out, Daryl has moved into the house with his family, it became unbearable to live there."

"Where are you living now?"

"With a lady that also works at Sonja's, she is renting me a room. I was thinking of seeing you before the holidays, I'll be spending Christmas with my son."

"Can you come for your birthday, Melie? I'd love to celebrate it here. I have the time now, in January I am going to be very busy, I'm starting a new job."

"How great, I have never been to DC, I'll come on my birthday weekend!"

"Chuck, I invited Melinda to come to celebrate her birthday with us here. You are going to meet an authentic, lively, spontaneous Gypsy girl."

Melinda came, I went to Union Station to pick her up. There she came running, shouting, full of joy, "Hi Sister! I'm here!"

She was wearing an embroidered, burgundy velvet coat, but she looked different.

"Your hair, Melie! You look so great, like when you were a little girl!"

"When I saw you, Lissa, with your light brown hair, so beautiful and classy, I remembered that was my natural color, and like when I was a little girl I wanted to be just like you. So after a few visits to the hairdresser to strip all that black color out, here I am. Looks natural, doesn't it?"

"Looks natural and beautiful, it is you, Melie!"

On the way home I drove by some of the monuments, she was in awe!

"DC is fabulous!"

Charles was pleasant and welcoming to her, we had dinner. Before he went to our room to do some work, he told her, "Melinda, tomorrow we are going to take you out for a very special dinner celebration at one of the most special restaurants in DC, but I want to know what you prefer, international cuisine, Mediterranean, Italian..."

"Charles, I am a burger and fries type of girl and I never go to fancy places."

"Do you like barbecue? Steak?"

"Yes, I love steak."

"I am making reservations at a Brazilian steakhouse, the best and finest you can find in DC, it is right on Pennsylvania Avenue, near the White House."

"That's a great choice, Chuck, but we need to go for an early dinner. It is a long course," I said.

Melinda jumped in:

"Lissa, a fine restaurant? Close to the White House? I have nothing to wear, look at my clothes, they are not what I would call elegant..."

"Don't worry, Melie, we are going shopping tomorrow, just for you, my birthday present!"

"How fun, it is so great to have my big sister back in my life. I feel so happy, Lissa! From now on, everything is going to be alright! You'll be proud of me."

"I am proud of you, but tell me about school. What do you want to do?"

"I dropped out of high school by the end of my junior year... I was getting married and honestly I was not the brightest student at all."

"Didn't they oppose you going to high school?"

"Mother and Father didn't say anything, I went because most of my friends were going too. But what do I do now? I am determined to go to fashion school and I need my high school diploma."

"If I were you, I would go to the high school and ask the counselor or the principal or both to finish your last year in a home program to complete all credits necessary to obtain your certificate."

"I didn't think of that, I'll try right after the holidays! How did you get yours?"

"I signed up for a GED program in Ohio, and in two years I got my certificate. That took me to the Community College and from there to the University."

"Oh, you had guts, Lissa! I don't want to spoil our time together, but I need to tell you just this once that I understand why you needed to come back to Princeton and do what you did. I respect your courage and admire you!"

"Thank you, Melie, I feel at peace with myself now."

Our following day was very exciting, we spent it shopping. Suzy had showed me stores in Northern Virginia, and I ended up buying clothes and toys for my nephew Timmy too. I hope to meet him someday soon.

I got Melie a very special dress for her birthday and a few extra things. She was excited like a little girl.

That evening Charles took us out for dinner, she raved about it! We had the greatest time, I felt an immense joy being with my little sister.

I visited Deborah to wish her happy holidays, she told me she was going to Aspen, Colorado, for the new year with a new friend.

"On a personal note, I met someone and things are going well. This time I was smart, found a man in my age range, also divorced, and we are doing very well together."

"I am glad to hear it, Deb! Is he a reporter?"

"Yes, a reputable one, he is with the Associated Press. You'll meet him one of these days... Things are looking up for me, Lissa."

"I wish you the very best, Deb. You are a wonderful friend. And I'm looking forward to spend a busy year collaborating with you."

"It is going to be a good year, fasten your seatbelt, Lissa!"

We haven't seen Kevin and Suzy since we returned from Iowa. They offered us a beautiful dinner party to celebrate our wedding, then they flew to Texas to spend the holidays with her family.

I said goodbye to my Chicago job with much gratitude for the opportunity that brought me to DC and into my brand new, beautiful life!

Charles and I are in love, so much love. This Christmas was blessed, we didn't want to go anywhere or be with anyone, just the two of us, close together in our little world, making plans for the family we are creating, loving one another.

Mom and Dad called us to wish us a Merry Christmas. Then we called again for New Year's!

I started the new job in January. What a challenging and exciting year we had ahead. The media was heating up, I was keeping my head cool.

I prepared a special dinner to celebrate the second anniversary of when we met. I couldn't wait for Charles to come home.
"Oh, Chuck, I want to give you the best present."
"My love, you gave it to me already, I have you, my life is complete."
"No, not yet, it will be complete after our baby is here. You are going to be a Daddy!"
"Really? A baby! When?" He hugged me, lifted me up. We never felt this happy before. "Thank you, darling."
"Our baby will come in the fall."
"How are you going to handle it with your new job? I don't want you getting overwhelmed."
"I'll be fine, I won't be travelling much. It will be alright!"
"Let's call my folks, they are going to be so excited!"

They were exultant.
"Chuck is going to be a Dad! We hope it is a granddaughter. We have two boys, two grandsons, it is time for a little girl!"
That day Dad told us that he will probably be coming to Washington in March, date still to be determined, for a meeting at the Department of Agriculture.

"Bring Mom, come and stay with us, we will show you around," Charles told him.

"How exciting, Chuck! I'd love to see them. Were they here before?"

"No, just Dad. It will be fun if Mom comes too this time."

Charles' parents came in March! We showed them around, took them for special dinners, and I was glad to have the opportunity to learn more about their responsibilities on the farm. They work hard, she assists the workers' families, and he is in charge of all the administrative execution.

Dad spoke passionately about his work:

"There are many challenges with the infrastructure, rural insurance, legislation for the workers and for the social and economic progress of the land and the products. I am also with the Soybean Farmers Association in Cedar Rapids, which consumes much time. I would like to partially retire from that someday.

We farmers have to be responsive to new circumstances that affect our fields, creating adequate conditions and laying the ground where the seeds grow. Working continuously and arduously we see the results of our labor. It is like a metaphor for life… Work hard and collect the results.

The farm is a continuous resource, the land will give back time after time. I'm proud of being part of the extensive cropland across the Great Plains."

Being with my parents-in-law opened my eyes to how much dedication they have for their farm, their livelihood.

It was heartwarming, for the first time I am experiencing the love of a united family.

Magdalene and I spent time alone. We went on a shopping spree, she was so enthusiastic about the winter sale and bought many items for Kristin and the boys. We bonded like mother and daughter, I don't remember having an experience like that with my own mother, ever.

I had the opportunity to tell her what happened with my family in West Virginia and of my dilemma between the truth and bringing my father to justice.

She was shocked but understood me.

"When you and Chuck told me that you had run away and had unfinished issues with your family, I immediately suspected it was about incest. But murder? That's unimaginable! How could a little girl deal with it?"

"There was extensive physical and mental abuse, beatings, name calling, anything to demean and dominate me... I tried to deal with it on my own, but it was not until Chuck came into my life that I really faced it and took responsibility to resolve it. I owed vindication to my Grandma Eden! After that, I could move on with my life."

"That was the only fair and just thing you could do, Lissa, for your grandmother and for yourself. It took a lot of courage, but now you can live this authentic and happy life. My son is a very lucky man for having married you."

My new job with Deborah was going well, I was growing in front of the cameras.

This summer we skipped the beach. I was becoming uncomfortable outside on the hot and sunny days.

Melinda and I were in constant contact and she made the decision to come to help me. Charles and I welcomed her into our home.

"Your sister is very pleasant and cheerful company, I am glad she will be here to help you."

Our baby was about to be born and I took maternity leave.

We knew we were having a girl, no one else knew until she was born.

Charles suggested naming our daughter Victoria! I love the name.

"It's a regal name, and Grandma Tori will be proud! Do you agree, Lis?"

"I agree, we should call our baby girl Vicki! And her middle name is Eden, Victoria Eden Hartsplend! Sounds good, doesn't it?"

Our Vicki, our beautiful, perfect baby girl came into the world at the end of September, our family was now complete! I felt an emotion like never before, holding my baby in my arms, it was like a miracle! I was blessed!

Charles, my Chuck, was beside himself.

"I am a Dad, our lives are changed, it is not you and me anymore, there is this little person, our daughter, for us to love and to hold … We are parents!"

The grandparents and great-grandmother celebrated at the farm. We will bring our baby girl for them to see her as soon as we could. They couldn't wait.

Mom told me she would have come to help me if I didn't have my sister, lately she won't leave the farm so she could be with Grandma Tori, who doesn't want to admit it, but needs constant company and assistance.

"But when you come, Lissa, bring your sister, we would love to meet her, she is part of the family too."

I returned to work in four weeks, and Melinda stayed in our apartment with Vicki. I had an agreement with my sister, she would help me with Vicki while she completes her credits for high school, which I was helping her with, to then apply to a fashion design institute.

Melinda did get approval from the school district to complete her senior year of high school in a homeschooling program. She was very determined.

She would be travelling frequently to West Virginia to see her son and to do her finals. When in Princeton she visited Mother.

"I don't like to be in her house anymore. Dylan is as rude and aggressive as Father was, the house is in disarray with all his children, and his wife doesn't get along with Mother. No one does, she is so bitter now."

"Melie, Mother should watch her back. If Dylan is anything like you are saying, and his wife does not get along with her, they might want the house all for themselves… What a horrible thought."

"I had the same thought, Lissa, and I truly want to keep a

distance from them… They are toxic."

We celebrated our first wedding anniversary on Thanksgiving with our baby. The family called us, but we were still debating if we should go for Christmas. They couldn't wait to hold Vicki.

On the line Magdalene was emotional.

"I want to hold her, she is so pretty, she looks like you, Chuck, when you were a baby, with the same reddish locks, but she has her Mom's blue eyes. My first granddaughter!"

We gave thanks for our love, our family unity.

In our room alone, with our little girl sleeping in the cradle, I hugged my husband. "Forever so grateful for all of our blessings, for all the love you brought into my life and the gift of a new life. It all came with you, my husband, my love."

"I am the happiest creature in the world. Perhaps other people have said so before, but not one with such justice."[*22]

I told my in-laws that I would be coming to the Iowa Caucus in February. They said they would meet me in Iowa City. Mom was so understanding, she told us that she thought Vicki was too young to travel in the winter for the holidays. She suggested, "Bring Vicki to Iowa City, Doug and I will take care of her while you work."

"Are you sure, Mom? Do you think Grandma Tori could come too?"

"Yes, that's not a long drive for us, it will be great to spend time with our granddaughter."

I agreed, Vicki would be four months old by then.

Melinda went to see her son.

We spent the holidays alone in our apartment, our first with our little girl. It was so sweet. That day, sitting around the Christmas tree with Vicki on my lap, I asked Charles if he ever thought to reconsider his work position, I would love to have him more available for us, for our family.

He told me he had been thinking the same, not right now but eventually he would seek some changes. I felt glad that family life and being with me and Vicki were important things to him.

"I need to balance my professional and personal life. I see that doing what we do we can still be good husbands and fathers, like Kevin with his children, he is present as much as he can be, but I can't deny that some time and some experiences are lost when we are away."

"Thank you for considering it, Chuck. Our baby girl only will benefit from having her Daddy around."

"And I don't want to miss anything, first steps, first words…"

Charles and I started our new year alone, dancing. Our life together is nothing but a dream… Sometimes I open my eyes to reality, I adore my husband, I have a wonderful marriage and the loveliest baby girl! I am in a good place in my career. 'Is this real?' My past struggles look so distant now… It is all fading away…

My partnership with Deborah was working perfectly. We made our plan of action and I gathered all my energy for this very challenging election year. The media was already in turmoil.

Melinda came back. I was glad to know that she is on good terms with her ex-husband and she spent an entire week with her son in his house. She also saw Mother.

"Lissa, Mother told me she never visited Father in prison and she never will. Surprisingly she is thankful to you, she feels liberated from him. By the way, she also said that she facilitated your escape from home for your own good, for you to have the life you wanted."

"Well, it's true that she turned a blind eye when I left, she gave me cash and left me alone in Princeton the day after I told her I was going to run away. I always thought she wanted to get rid of me, I was a liability…"

"Mother said she regrets what happened when she realized you had told the truth, she became afraid of him and did not stand up for you. She wants your forgiveness."

"Melie, I have reasons not to believe her, you lived with her longer than I did… Do you think she is being sincere?"

"She is, maybe you should give her a chance to explain herself.

She said she is proud of you and what you have accomplished."

"I don't nurture ill feelings towards Mother, I let it all go… I'll never go back to Princeton. To be honest I do not have a bond with Mother, and right now I don't feel like seeing her, but I won't rule it out, maybe someday…"

"I suggest you meet Mother in Martinsburg, she is moving in with Mira. It's only a little over an hour away from DC, and I bet Mira would love to see you again."

"Oh, Miranda! She never cared for me, she practically ignored me, I never felt I had an older sister. How is she?"

"You'll be surprised, Mira and Mother look so much alike, like older sisters, I mean Mira looks so much older than you, than us. We are the younger sisters!"

"Sisters, Melie, for always. I'm proud of you, Baby Sister. You are a peacemaker and very talented."

"I feel so lucky to have you back, Lissa. With your help I am moving forward, I'll be getting my certificate this year and I am searching for fashion schools, there are a few. I'll get there, it will cost money, but I figure I can waitress at the side to support myself."

"Melie, you can and I will help you, I'll pay for the tuition, I'll give you a scholarship!"

"Thank you, Lissa, you have been my biggest supporter, you are my inspiration, you made it all by yourself, I can't imagine how difficult it was for you, I will follow your example."

"What about your son? Moving further away, you'll see less of him. How do you feel about that?"

"I will visit my Timmy as often as I can. He is five years old and now he understands that I love him and he'll always be part of my life. The last time I saw him I asked, if he had to choose, which parent he would like to live with. Without hesitation, he responded, 'With Daddy!' I hugged him and told him I understand he loves his Daddy.

He said, 'I love you too, Mommy, but I have the most fun with my Daddy.' I have to recognize that Tim Ray and I were not a good match, but he is a dedicated father, and because I love my son I'll let him be happy the way he chooses. Someday I hope he understands!"

"That is unselfish of you, Melie."

I went to Iowa for the caucus in February and brought Vicki along. Charles couldn't come, he was away on another trip. Douglas, Magdalene and Grandma Tori came to see us in Iowa City, as they promised. They reserved a large suite for us to stay together. So nice having them around!

Mom held Vicki, "She is all mine for three days!"

Grandma Tori was delighted, "Thank you for naming her after me, it is an honor. My first great-granddaughter!"

I invited Dad to come along with me to the caucus, he loved it! He is well informed about politics and likes to be involved.

We had a heart to heart talk. He said that since Charles left the family to go to the military he supported his son's decision, but his heart was broken seeing his boy going to war.

"I hope that being mature and married to you and having a baby, Charles will settle down. Growing up he was a daredevil, fearless, and he placed that energy into being a Marine. I can tell you now that during those years I lived in anguish, afraid that one day my son was going to be sent back home in casket. It was a horrible feeling. Now with the job he has at the Pentagon, and all those trips that he takes around the world, I'm afraid that he continues being exposed to daring situations. Does he tell you anything about it, Lissa?"

"No, he can't tell, his job is Top Secret, but Chuck assures me that he is always safe, he is not on the front lines, his meetings abroad are in safe locations. That's all I know, I believe he is safe."

"Only you can ground him, Lissa, he loves you, and now especially having Vicki, I bet my son will reconsider the kind of job that takes him away from his family."

"I hope so too, Dad. I miss him so much when he is away and I have to confess that I also worry."

"Everything will work out for the best, Lissa, I have faith."

Mom delighted herself taking care of Vicki, who couldn't stop smiling at her loving Grandma. I saw a clear bond that would never be broken. My Vicki will grow up being loved by all of us.

"You and Chuck didn't take the time to come to Kohler yet. Try this summer, I am going to spend time with my sister there. She has come to see me a few times at the farm, but it never coincided when you were there. Please come to meet Adelaide."

"I'll try, Mom, this is a very challenging year, I'll do my best. You talk lovingly about your sister, I'd love to know more about her. Does she live in that same area in Wisconsin?"

"Adelaide lives in Jefferson County. She still works with my father's business, he was a dairy products wholesale broker.

She and I went to school in Milwaukee, she did business and I went into social services. After graduating she went back home to join the family business, I stayed in Milwaukee with a government job as a social worker."

"So neither one of you came from a farmer's background? How did you meet Dad? Were you in Iowa?"

"No, we were at a beach resort on vacation, my sister and I, and Doug was there with some friends. We connected. He came to see me often in Milwaukee, it is only a four hour drive from the farm... Then he brought me to meet his parents, I fell in love with them and the land, but I debated with myself when he proposed. I loved him, but it was very hard to leave Wisconsin, my family, my job in Milwaukee.

My sister, who is a strong woman, was my biggest supporter, my rock, I saw her often and we always spent time with our children at the beaches, the gorgeous Lake Michigan beaches..."

"By the way, I love her name, Adelaide... And I have seen one of the beaches from the distance once when I went to Milwaukee for a convention... It reminded me of the Chicago beaches, they are by the same lake! And I would love to spend more time there with you and your family, even if it is only for a weekend."

When I returned to DC I told Charles about his father's concerns. "He has worried about you for so long, Chuck..."

"I know, occasionally I feel guilty, but I truly believe in what I do."

"Chuck, I worry too, sometimes I wish you were not involved with national security, terrorism... I wish."

He hugged me and kissed me, reassuring me that we will always be fine.

"Mom asked us to come to Wisconsin, to the beach resort in the summer, she is getting together with her sister. It is important to her, and I would love to meet your aunt. Let's see if we can arrange at least a weekend to do that, instead of going to North Carolina."

"I think it is possible, you would love to meet Aunt Adele! She is a businesswoman, but kind and sweet like Mom, they even sound alike."

At work my partnership with Deborah was supportive, we had a good understanding, but lately we were at low point in American journalism, and the public is not getting the accurate narrative. In some cases there is a display of dishonesty from some individuals and also some politicians misleading the public to a level of hysteria, some guests on the show start shouting blatantly. It is a disgrace when commonplace and stale remarks are being used only for the sake of ratings and headlines.

Deborah and I are getting frustrated, and there is still a long way to go!

Melinda stayed with Vicki while I had to work at the conventions in the summer. After I returned she went to be with Timmy for a week.

Charles and I were able to take a few days off, and we went to Wisconsin with our baby girl to meet Mom and Aunt Adele.

I was surprised when we arrived at Kohler, a splendid resort by Andrae State Park. Happy to see that Grandma Tori came along!

"I wouldn't miss a chance to see my little, only great-granddaughter. Oh, she is so pretty!"

"We are happy to see you too, Grandma!"

I was very pleased to meet Aunt Adele. As Charles had told me, she resembled his mother and also sounded like her, just a bit older, a strong, intelligent woman.

"Couldn't wait to meet you, Lissa! Magda talks so much about you, she is proud of you!"

During our conversation Aunt Adele told me that she is a

divorced widow.

"I mean, my husband divorced me, but a few years later he died... I always wanted to have a marriage like my sister Magda and Doug have, but that was not meant to be for me, so I resigned myself to being a mother and a working woman, I still didn't let go of the business and I work side by side with my older son."

In another opportunity she told me that she had lost a son, her middle child. He was born with cerebral palsy and lived until he was twenty nine years old.

"I was very dedicated to him, that was the reason for my divorce... But I don't regret it at all, now when I think of him, I smile. He lived the life he was meant to live, and I loved him unconditionally, I still do."

"That's very comforting when we have the peace of mind knowing that we did our best for the ones we love, Aunt Adele."

I could see the clear bond that these two sisters have, Magdalene and Adelaide! They went through life supporting one another, away but close at heart... The three of us went for long walks at the amazing golden beach with incredible sand dunes.

"This is the largest dune complex along Wisconsin's coastline."

They told me stories of years ago when their children were young and they would meet at that resort in the summer. Charles had great memories of that time spent with his cousins. Memories, memories... Isn't that all we are left with?

"The experiences of today are the memories of tomorrow! We better make good and happy memories..."

The days of relaxing with the family were amazing, it restored us. Mom took Vicki for an evening and gave Charles and me a night out by ourselves.

"Have a romantic night!" she told us.

We did. Sometimes, having a baby, it is so easy to be wrapped up in being Mom and Dad, we valued time to be husband and wife.

I wish we could have stayed longer.

Again this year it will be impossible to come to the Fall Festival, it's an election year... I am so busy. But I promised to make time to nurture our relationship and I also would love to see Aunt Adele again. She might join us at the farm next time.

On our flight back to DC I talked to Charles about how I have been feeling about my job. Although I love working with Deborah, I'm disappointed with the media environment in general. It has been a struggle to maintain our work ethic among so much controversy and biased judgments surrounding us.

"Sometimes I think my work is in vain and I would be better off applying my skills writing about something else more meaningful."

"I understand, I can see what is going on. Are you having any regrets working in political broadcasting?"

"I think so, politics was not my passion, it was the opportunity given to me and I embraced it, but there are other things I could write about ..."

"Whatever you want to do, darling, I will support you. I also have been thinking more about my job. The secrecy that I am committed to, it started bothering me, sometimes I want to share something with you, and I can't. We share all of our thoughts and feelings, but my work. I might look into a different position..."

"I appreciate that, Chuck, and as you just told me... Whatever you want to do, I will support you."

Mom came to DC for Vicki's first birthday in October. Wonderful surprise!

"My only granddaughter, I couldn't miss it."

She met Melinda and they had a good time while I was intensely working overtime.

"Sorry, Mom, this time I can't go out with you."

"I understand, don't worry, I am having a good time with your sister. She is so spontaneous, she has a childlike appreciation for things, she is delightful company and I see how she treats Vicki, so much love!"

"Melie is good-hearted, loving and talented. I am proud of her."

Election Day! The media was in turmoil, I worked until two in the morning. Charles sent me a driver to bring me home. He is so protective!

"No way you are coming home alone."

In the morning I could breathe again. It was over! I was working from home, in my pajamas all day, holding my baby girl.

Douglas called me, "I told you I was going to talk to you after the election, what do you think of the results, Lissa?"

"I'm not surprised, Dad! It was an open game, anything could happen."

Douglas and I had a long conversation, I knew the candidates up close. We talked for hours.

In the end he told me, "I can see why my son loves you, you are fair, level-headed and smart, I'm glad you are my daughter!"

"My father-in-law is my new best friend, a farmer from Iowa, we have so much in common, I spent hours on the phone with him today," I told Charles when he came home.

"My father is under your spell too, another Hartsplend that loves you!"

"Chuck! You gave me love and a family, all that I wished for! Thank you, my love."

This year we went to the farm for the holidays and we stayed until New Year's. I'm so glad we did it, we had the most delightful time with our family.

Ryan and Josh wanted to take our little girl on her first sleigh rides, Charles supervised them and they had great fun. Vicki, now fourteen months old, wouldn't stop giggling.

Charles and I watched the deepest dark blue, starry night sky, sitting out on the freezing porch, contemplating the most amazing view of the fields, fully covered in glistening snow.

Great-Grandma Tori and Grandma Magda stayed with 'their little Vicki' almost all the time.

At ninety two Grandma Tori didn't show the same energy, but she was still lively and hopeful.

"To wish was to hope, and to hope was to expect."[23]

She told me, "It's winter, I'll be more energetic in the spring. I had a beautiful, long life, I am in peace and harmony, surrounded by the love of my family, but I am not ready yet, I still have one more wish... I hope to see my grandson Charles and his family back in this beautiful place, then I'll go, leaving behind nothing but loving memories."

CHAPTER SEVEN

UNISON

*B*ack in DC on Inauguration Day, January 2017...

"It has been four years since we met at the Inaugural Ball, four years! Look how much has happened. We fell in love, we are married and have a beautiful daughter, my love. Who could have predicted it?"

"Not me, Chuck, I feel so lucky and so much in love with you."

"Do you want to go dancing and start over again, darling?"

"We'll dance right here in our home! The music theme this time is also very fitting for us: *'My way! I did it my way!'*"

Charles and I discussed having another baby.

"We are so happy with one... What about giving Vicki a little brother or a little sister? But first I think we should consider moving into a house with more space, a little yard. What do you think, darling?"

"I would love that, and the idea of buying a house makes me happy, settled. You know how I feel about being permanent!"

"I agree, would you mind living in Arlington? That neighborhood where Kevin and Suzy live is pretty good and they like the local schools. Let's make our new project for this new year to buy a house."

Suzy got very excited with the news that we could eventually become neighbors.

Charles and I started looking for a house, but it didn't seem it was working for us for one reason or another. We put it on hold until Charles returned from one of his trips.

The year started and it continued to be tumultuous professionally, didn't get much better as time went on. Deborah and I made a strong alliance maintaining our show respected and respectable. We got positive feedback from our audience.

"Deb, I read an article by one of the best, old school journalists in the country and he commented that 'the honorable and respected profession of journalism is dying.' In its place there is a pack of unscrupulous individuals disrespecting what's true and honest, and that the few who stand by their values are under pressure from the rest of the media and special interest groups. What do you think is going to happen?"

"History will tell us. Let's keep in mind that most of those commentators are not true journalists, they are feeding on muddy rhetoric only for the sake of ratings and headlines. But if we stand on fairness and good judgment, sooner or later the truth will prevail."

"I agree with you, Deb!"

I was in the office on a warm spring afternoon when I heard from the Associated Press that an American compound in Sudan had been attacked by terrorists. There were casualties, but the Pentagon didn't disclose any names yet.

Deborah came in. "Did you hear, Lissa?"

"I did, Deb, it keeps happening... This news always makes me feel sick."

Unexpectedly Charles called me. He was very somber and spoke in an unusually low voice:

"Lissa, there was an attack in Sudan."

"I just heard it, Chuck. I'm so glad you are home!"

"Kevin was in Sudan, in a meeting in that compound..."

"Kevin? Don't, please don't say it, Chuck. Please, it has to be a mistake..."

I was shaking, everything became blurred. My heart skipped a beat... *'Kevin was there!'*

"I am sorry to tell you, Kevin is among the victims. Lissa, we need to help Suzy, it is going to be on the news... I'm going to her house with an officer now, please meet me there."

I was numb, in an alternate state of reality.

I talked to Deborah, "I need to go, our friend Kevin was one of the victims and I need to help Suzy, his wife."

Then I called Melinda, "I am glad you are home with Vicki, I'll be late today…"

When I arrived at Suzy's home, Charles was already there with an officer.

Suzy was crying. I held her. She didn't say a word, she didn't have to, there were no words to be said…

Her children were at a neighbor's house.

I looked at Charles with compassion. He was devastated, he lost his friend and he had a job to do.

"The officer and I have to remove everything from Kevin's office."

"I don't understand, why?" Suzy asked him.

"It's part of the protocol, we have to remove files... I'm sorry, Suzy."

There was a hole in my chest, a knot in my throat when Suzy started screaming out loud, "Kevin, my love, come home, come back to us!"

After the officer left with boxes of Top Secret files, a computer, phones, Charles gave her an envelope. "Kevin left it for you, Suzy."

The envelope was addressed: 'To my beloved wife Suzy.' She did not open it.

Charles spoke to Kevin's parents.

The phone was ringing, I picked up all the calls. One of them was Suzy's mother from Dallas to tell her daughter she was coming on the first flight to be with her and watch the children.

"What can I do, Suzy? How can I soften your pain, my dear friend?"

Later, Kevin's sister and brother-in-law showed up, they picked up Kev Junior and Emma from the neighbor's house, and Suzy told me, "His sister and I have to tell the children that Daddy is not coming home…"

We gave the family privacy.

Charles and I went home to our daughter. We didn't speak all the way.

Our little girl ran to us, all cheerful in her innocence, "Mama! Dada!"

We both held her and we cried.

Never saw Charles crying… And here he was in agony, vulnerable. We comforted each other with our love.

The next morning Suzy's parents and brother arrived.

Charles discussed the arrangements for the burial at Arlington Cemetery. Suzy and Kevin's father agreed.

"My son should be with heroes like him."

Three days went by, all I wanted was to not feel any more pain, fear and anger. I was very angry at the world, at terrorists, and at politicians who are nothing but talk…

Suzy told me, "I feel like someone just ripped my heart out of my chest in cold blood. I want my husband, the father of my children, back!"

We accompanied Suzy and family to the ceremonies.

At the base we sat in an open hangar, the airplane was parked on the tarmac. One by one they brought out four caskets covered with the American flag.

The President and officials spoke words of praise and gratitude for their sacrifice and service to the country.

We proceeded to Arlington for the ceremonial burial. And late in the afternoon, it was all over!

Suzy and her family went back to her home in deepest sorrow.

Charles and I spent the day together, discussing our emotions and feelings, we were both devastated.

I told him, "I took what happened to Kevin very personally, it is hurting me badly, I can't imagine being in that situation. That letter from Kevin that you gave Suzy… Was it a goodbye letter? Did you ever write one like that, Chuck?"

"Yes, darling, we are encouraged to leave a message to our wives, just in case…"

I cried, "I will never read a letter like that, never! I can't think of ever losing you so violently and abruptly. What would be the purpose to tell me that you loved me and our daughter, but you loved your job more?"

He hugged me and cried, "I can't imagine abandoning you and our little girl this way either. I will not abandon you, I have seen much death and destruction, all for the sake of peace… I'm tired, Lis, I'm tired of this."

"Rest, my love, rest. I'm so sorry you lost one more friend, one more hero! I never want to bury you at Arlington with all ceremony to be called a hero, not you, Chuck, you belong with us, with your family."

For a few days Charles didn't talk about it, but he was visibly consumed by the tragic event.

I felt sick, lost interest in my work, all that chatter going around seemed meaningless. Deborah offered me a leave of absence, I took only a few days to spend more time with Suzy. I visited her every day, her father and brother returned to Texas, but her mother stayed with her.

"Lissa, I made a decision, I am waiting for the end of the school year and I'll be moving back home to Texas in the summer. I can't stay around here in Arlington, close to the Pentagon… Promise you'll come to see me there."

"I will, Suzy, I'll miss you, but I am glad you are going to be with your family, and it is good for the children, they'll have a new start."

"I am counting also on my brother, he is a caring uncle. Kev Junior and Emma will have the love and guidance of a father…"

I recognized she made the best decision, but I felt sad, I'll be losing the closeness of her friendship... My heart ached for her, she lost much more than that.

I came back to work and unexpectedly I got a call from Sunjay! Strangely enough I thought of him recently. Seeing how affected Charles was by the death of his best friend, I remembered how the death of Sunjay's friend propelled him into following the path his family chose for him...

'How can something tragic like this happen again?'

"Lissa, this is Sunjay from Pittsburgh. Do you remember me?"

"Sunjay! What a surprise!"

"I hope you don't mind I'm calling you, I have seen you on TV and it was easy to locate you."

"I am truly surprised, Sunjay! How are you? Are you in DC?"

"Yes, I am here at a conference and was hoping I could see you. I have missed you all of these years, about fifteen years... Do you remember us?"

"I remember you, of course, but we moved on, both of us built new lives, I can't meet you. Do you still live in New Jersey?"

"No, I moved to California, Silicon Valley, years ago. I know you are a successful journalist, but I want to know if you are happy with your life."

"I am married to a wonderful man and I have a little girl that I adore, I am happy, my life turned out for the best, but I never forgot how you helped me at the Community College, I am grateful to you, Sunjay."

"That's all you feel, gratitude? I loved you, Lissa, truly loved you. I have questioned my decision of honoring my family's wishes. I married the woman they chose, had three children, but I am alone now. When I was recruited for a major position in Silicon Valley, she didn't want to follow me. She is a good person, a dedicated mother, but there was not an emotional connection between us, I never had for her the feelings I had for you, it was once in a lifetime..."

"Thank you for saying that, Sunjay, you were my first love. I was a girl when we met, and you didn't leave anything but good memories of our young, impossible love affair."

"Lissa, when I left I didn't say goodbye... I only told you I had to follow my destiny. You didn't hold me back, I never forgot your beautiful blue eyes welling up with tears while you were wishing me happiness. I know I caused you pain and I am truly sorry."

"You don't have to apologize, I understood and knew that you had to go. We may say goodbye now, but know that I wish you nothing but love and happiness."

"Thank you, Lissa. I wish you all the best, my first, unforgettable love."

I stayed at my desk, reflecting for a moment on what just happened. *'Was that serendipity?'* I realized that when we love someone that feeling remains in a corner of our heart, even when there is no room for that person in our life any longer. It was love, young, immature love.

After a few days my sister approached me.

"I'm sorry, Lissa, I have seen you so sad and I don't know what to say. Are you afraid for Charles? You worry about his job, don't you?"

"Yes, Melie, I worry and I am in pain for what happened to Kevin and for Suzy… Life is not fair, is it? But I am here for you too and very grateful that you are taking care of Vicki, she is happy with you."

"Like I was when I was little and you took care of me. I love Vicki so much."

"Changing subjects, how are your studies coming along?"

"I have to thank you too, Lissa, you made it all possible, I need to go back to finish my tests and get my certificate, and I am looking forward to start school in the fall. But sometimes I doubt myself, I am afraid that people would be prejudicial about my style and for being Gypsy, and I will not have a chance to succeed."

"Don't worry, Melie, honor your origin, your particular taste and style, bring the colors of your roots out into the world, just be yourself. Be bold, people will respect you and love you for who you are and you'll succeed."

"There is something else I need to tell you… Dylan went to see Father in prison and he was told that his health situation is critical, it got worse, now he has liver cancer, he is being treated, but looks like he has not much time left…"

"Well, that was expected, I just wish that he makes peace with himself before… Are you going to visit him? Have you spoken to Mother about this?"

"I am not going to see him, but I pray for him. And Mother is not going either, she said she is totally detached from him. Talking about fathers, I have news about Tim Ray, he is moving to Charleston. He is getting married and has a new job there."

"Married? How do you feel about that?"

"I think it is great, he is happier now and he is giving me more time with Timmy, and also his move is making my choice of fashion school easier… I was deciding between Philadelphia, Pennsylvania or Columbus, Ohio.

First I need to be accepted, but I think Columbus will be ideal! I can travel on I-77 to get to Charleston faster."

"Indeed! How ironic, that is the route I took to Ohio when I ran away from home."

"I think you were so brave, you were young and alone, your courage gave me the strength to follow my dream. Because of you, Lissa, I'll be on my own, but sometimes I lack confidence and I am afraid it won't work."

"Believe in yourself, you can do it!"

Melinda took off to West Virginia to see her son and to get her certificate!

She is going on with her life. I am proud of my sister!

For almost two weeks Charles hasn't been talking about the last events. He has spent some time quietly. I gave him space to reflect, he needs to come to terms and make a decision about his life, our lives.

Finally he was ready to talk to me.

"Thank you, my love, for understanding and giving me the time to reflect. For half of my life I dedicated myself to our country, to protect and preserve the peace, to fight terrorism. I saw many calamities and many deaths, until this last one, the loss of my friend hurt me deeply. I saw his family's pain. Suzy and his children's devastation is something I would never ever want to inflict on you, on our daughter and my family.

I have come to realize that twenty years of service is a good enough contribution and I speculate the possibility of changing my job position at the Pentagon. But what I really want for the next twenty and the next… is to be dedicated to our marriage, raising our daughter and then growing old together."

"Oh Chuck, my love. I wanted so much to hear these words. I have some news for you, it is not only Vicki. We have another baby on the way, I am pregnant!"

"Why didn't you tell me? Another baby!" He smiled and kissed me over and over.

"I didn't want to put any pressure on you, Chuck. You are going to be a Daddy again."

"It is wonderful, the right time! What I really want is to go back to my roots, to the farm. My father has far too many responsibilities with the farm's administration and the association in Cedar Rapids. Colin is an expert in farming, he manages the workers and knows the land so well, he can teach me quite a lot about it.

I thought of moving back to Iowa, but I have been afraid that you wouldn't like to live there because of your career and I know how much you like this area."

"You know how I feel about my career, Chuck. I can write from anywhere, I can get a freelance contract with the network. It is true that I love DC, here is where my life ascended, where we met, where our daughter was born. I love the energy of the city, the monuments, the museums, but I would trade everything to live with you anywhere in this world, I love the farm and your family. Chuck, I think it is perfect! Did you talk to your parents yet? They will be so happy!"

"No, I was waiting to talk to you first, we'll call them together. Dad is seventy now and has been talking about reducing his load, having more time for the grandchildren, I'm sure he will welcome my help. I also feel it is a good move to reframe my relationship with Colin.

And I'll build us the most beautiful new house with everything you want, and I am also thinking we should get an apartment in Cedar Rapids. I'll be going there often and we can have some cultural outings and getaways for the two of us…

Lis, we will have a good life with our children there, and I'll go from saving the world to feeding the world…"

"Oh Chuck, this is it! You are speaking with so much joy! I feel happy with the prospect of creating roots, growing a garden…"

Charles couldn't contain his enthusiasm. We called Douglas and Magdalene.

"Dad, I've decided to quit my job and go back home. Do you still want me to be part of the family business? I will contribute!"

Doug broke into tears with the startling news!

"My son, I finally hear what I have been waiting for, for so long, you have your place here. I am slowing down, I'll delegate to you most of my responsibilities. Colin will be happy to have your collaboration too. Come home soon!"

Magdalene got to the phone already crying.

"We have something else to tell you, Mom, we are having another baby!"

"That's wonderful, can't wait to see you all here. When are you coming?"

"It will take a few of months to resolve everything with our jobs, the apartment. You can start planning, I am also planning to build a house for us."

"We will help with everything. In the meantime you'll stay with us in the main house, we have plenty of room. Let me run to tell Grandma Tori, can't imagine how happy she is going to be."

Later on, Colin called Charles back, "I heard the good news, Chuck, and I want to tell you I am happy you are coming home with your family, we will work well together. Welcome home, brother!"

"Thank you, Colin, it means so much to me. I want to make it up to you for your hard work all these years. You, Kristin, and if you want the boys too, are going on a trip, a long deserved trip wherever you want, here in the U.S. or abroad.

I have thousands of frequent flyer points, they are all yours, my gift! Make your plans!"

Colin got very excited, "This is so unexpected, I will tell Kristin, she is going to love it. Thank you, Chuck."

The Hartsplend family had a big celebration on the farm.

"We'll be reunited soon, working together, raising our children…"

Charles asked me, "What about Melinda? Did she decide where she is going?"

"She is going to Columbus, Ohio, she is starting fashion school in the fall. I am happy she is also going on with her life."

I told Melie about our move and she supported me.

"That's good news, Lissa. You and your family all together, but I'll miss you and Vicki, and I also want to see my new baby niece or nephew."

"Melie, you are my family, don't forget that, you are coming to visit us, and I would love if you could bring Timmy to spend vacations at the farm, it is a wonderful place, there is much for a boy to do there, he would love it. Do you think that is possible? Would Tim allow you?"

"I think so, Tim Ray has mellowed with me, I am sure he would let me take Timmy on a trip to visit my family. As we are talking about family, may I ask you, Lissa… Are you going to see Mother before you leave?"

"I am not planning to, Melie, I feel so detached from her. Maybe someday I will feel differently…"

"It was not your fault, Lissa, she was not really a mother to you, she was powerless, totally dominated by him. I understand how you feel and believe Mother does too."

*"She was without any power, because she was without any desire of command over herself."*24

"You always use quotes in the right moments, do they come from Grandma Eden?"

"My time with Grandma was very short-lived… I was too young to remember much of what she said, but I held on to the feelings, the love, her interest in books, reading and talking about them. She was reading *Pride and Prejudice* for me before she died, I couldn't understand much of what she was saying, but I was fascinated by her soft voice and laughed at the voices and accents that she would make up for the characters. It was fun... just fun.

I kept the book, and it was not until years later after I bought a dictionary that I could understand all the words, and like her, fell in love with Jane Austen's books and read them all and many other ones from the same era. That was my way of keeping Grandma's presence in my life, repeating the quotes that she appreciated...

You know how important it is for a child to grow up being loved, and she was the only one that truly loved me. Because of her and what she taught me, I became the person that I am."

"I feel emotional just listening, I wish I had known Grandma Eden, you looked up to her. I want you to know, Lissa, I look up to you, you made me believe in myself, you are my role model, and I told that to our mother."

"Oh my! Maybe she didn't like to hear it."

"She agreed with me, she said you were just like her mother. You had the same personality and the most beautiful blue eyes... It sounds crazy, but I think Mother was envious of Grandma and of you..."

I discussed with my friend Deborah our decision of moving away from Washington, DC.

"Deb, working with you has been a life-changing experience, I'll miss it. You gave me the greatest professional opportunity and I will always be grateful to you, but I need to leave.

Charles and I are moving to Iowa, we are going home. I want you to know that more than anything I value your friendship and my heart is broken for leaving, but I have the biggest reason for this, my Charles and my family.

I'm sorry, Deb, if it helps I can stay for the summer while you go on your vacation."

"I'll miss you dearly, Lissa, but I am happy for you and your family. Yes, it will help if you stay for the summer. I am sad to see you leaving. Wait! We can still work together, you can be our correspondent... Would you like to be the voice from the Heartland?"

"Yes, I would. I am thinking of getting freelance work in Cedar Rapids, I will continue writing."

"Great, Lissa, we will work long distance and we will meet at the next Iowa caucuses."

"Thank you, Deb, I am looking forward to continue our professional relationship, but most of all, our friendship. I will miss you, and whenever you want a place to relax, come to visit us, the farm is beautiful, you can't see a starry sky or breathe the purest air anywhere else!"

"The distance is nothing when one has a motive..."*25

School was over, and I went to Suzy to say goodbye.

"I will be in touch with you, I'll never forget you and the children, and I would love to see you in Iowa someday. Hope life is kinder to you, Suzy, time will heal your heart."

"I'll miss you, Lissa, and I am glad that Charles made this decision, at least something positive came out of Kevin's loss, his best friend realized that life with his family is more important than anything else."

"Charles had been brewing thoughts of leaving the Pentagon for a while, but the tragic loss was the catalyst, it was the last drop, he is still heartbroken for Kevin."

"It hurt us all. I have been here for over a decade, built a beautiful life with Kevin... He is gone, and I am leaving feeling defeated, I am embarking into the unknown, back to where I came from. Thank God I have my family to help me start over..."

My heart hurt for my dear friend Suzy, but I knew she was resilient and I was hopeful she would find her way to happiness. I prayed for her.

Doug called Charles, his enthusiasm comes through the phone lines and makes us smile! It is like the news about our move gave him a new life.

"Guess what I found... An apartment in Cedar Rapids, at one of the new buildings by the river bank that reminds me of yours by the Potomac! You will not miss that view. I am going to buy it!"

"But Dad, I was going to do it when we get there."

"I thought it was a good idea, I don't know why I never thought of that before. We go to Cedar Rapids so often for meetings, doctor's appointments, entertainment. And I want Lissa to have a comfortable place close to the hospital for the new baby's birth."

"Thank you, Dad, that is so thoughtful of you."

"And tell Lissa that Grandma Tori can't wait for her arrival, she is going to spoil her little great-granddaughter and she is happy to have another little one around here soon..."

The next day Magdalene called me.

"Lissa, I want to talk to you about Dad. Is Chuck home?"

"No, he is not, Mom, what is it?"

"First I need to tell you that the announcement of your move here brought a new hope to all of us, but mostly to Doug."

"It is a new life for all of us, Mom. What is happening to Dad?"

"He doesn't want me to tell anything to Chuck, he did not want to be an influence on Chuck's decisions, but Doug is suffering from a heart condition for the past two years. We have seen a specialist in Cedar Rapids frequently. He has atrial fibrillation and he is taking medication to keep it under control. He is doing well, more so now."

"Oh, we had no idea! I am so sorry, I imagine how worried you have been. Mom, we will help any way we can to make Dad feel better."

"You are helping already, he is so happy, a weight has been lifted off his shoulders, he is looking forward to having a long life surrounded by the family, and he is planning to pass on to Chuck all of his executive and administrative responsibilities."

"And Chuck is looking forward to working side by side with Dad and Colin, and I totally agree with him."

"Lissa, I also want to talk about you. I know how your career is important, you have a voice in the Washington media and I presume that this move is going to be very difficult to you. I want to offer you all of my support, I'll do anything you need to make this change in your professional life as soft as possible. Count on me, please. Because of you, our son is coming back to us. I love you."

"Thank you, Mom, thank you for understanding. I support Chuck's decision and I am happy we are joining the family, but I can tell you that it is bittersweet for me. I love Washington, my job and the life that we built here..." I cried, "Sorry, Mom, I am hormonal..."

"That's why I wanted to talk to you, Lissa, I understand, I put myself in your shoes and I clearly remember how painful my move to Iowa was when I married Doug... I loved my city of Milwaukee, I loved the beaches by the immense lake, and my job was very fulfilling. Most of all I had my family close by...

I loved Doug dearly, Grandma Tori was wonderful to me, always treated me like her own daughter, but I still missed what I had before. Took me a few years to adapt to life here. Adelaide, my sister, helped me, coming to visit, and in the summer months we would meet at the resort there. Then as time went by I got used to it, I started volunteering to help the workers' families, my boys were growing up and whenever I missed my old life, I went back to visit..."

"Mom, I have lived in many places and adapted to many circumstances, I am sure I'll be happy there, I have my family and that's all that matters. I am looking forward to spend time with you, Grandma Tori and everyone. And once in a while we can go places... For instance I love Chicago, I lived there, and it is only a three hour drive from Iowa. We can go together to enjoy it... Don't you think so?"

"Absolutely, Lissa, we will have some girl time at the Magnificent Mile shops, it will be fun. I also want to tell you that I have contacted the doctors at the hospital clinic and got the forms to transfer your records here. You are going to be well taken care of when the baby arrives, no worries."

"Thank you for thinking of everything, Mom. We will be reunited soon."

I spoke to Charles:

"Dad has a heart condition, he is under treatment for a while, but he didn't want you to know. Mom told me that lately he is very upbeat, your decision is impacting him in a very positive way."

"My Dad is such a strong man, I admire him and I am glad we are going to make a difference in their lives."

"Chuck, talking to your Mom makes me feel like she is my real mother and I started feeling like I do not want to leave behind unresolved issues with my own mother, I should see her one last time to say goodbye. Would you mind in coming to Martinsburg? Melie is stopping at my sister Miranda's house on her way to

Charleston before moving to Columbus."

"I'll be glad to, we'll drop Melie off, and you can talk to your mother, and I'll have the chance to meet her for once."

Melinda helped enormously in getting rid of many of our things and packing items that we sent in advance to the farm. We left in the apartment only essential pieces of furniture.

I gave her many of my dresses, and she took almost all of my high heels.

"I don't need this much anymore, I am not going to be in front of the cameras every day..."

She was getting ready to leave when I surprised her.

"Chuck and I are going to drop you off in Martinsburg, I want to see Mother one last time, but don't tell her. I don't want her to prepare anything. We won't stay long."

"Lissa, this is fantastic! Did you forgive her? I am so glad you are coming."

"I will never forget what she did, how she raised me and didn't protect me as a child, but I don't hold on to resentment, I freed myself from the past and I want her to know that."

Melie hugged me and we cried. "Lissa, you are the best person I know, I am so proud you are my sister. I am going to miss you and Vicki so much."

"Melie, I will always be your big sister and no matter how far we are, we will always be together, I will be following your progress and rejoicing in your successes. And remember you are always welcome in my house, you and your son!"

On a warm morning we left for Martinsburg. On the way there, Melie, sitting in the back seat close to Vicki, told Charles:

"Chuck, Mother is going to be impressed! I am sure she never met a distinguished man like you... I had told her that my sister married a handsome gentleman, and I am proud of being your sister-in-law. I want you to know that you always made me feel welcomed and comfortable in your home. Thank you!"

He smiled at her, "Thank you, Melie, you are endearing!"

I looked at my husband, "Distinguished, handsome gentleman, love of my life!"

"I am the lucky one, my lovely, gorgeous wife!"

We arrived at Miranda's house in one of the nicest neighborhoods in Martinsburg.

Melinda ran to the front door and we waited in the SUV. She came back with my older sister, for a moment I thought I was seeing my mother some years younger... Miranda was very friendly.

"What a surprise! Why didn't you tell us you were coming, Lissa? Please come in."

I introduced her to my husband and Vicki, sleeping in the car seat. Charles carried her and we walked into the house.

"Miranda, we are not staying long, I just want to see Mother... Is she here?"

"Yes, she is in her room in the basement."

Melie immediately said, "I'm going to bring her upstairs."

Mira made some short conversation.

"Your daughter is so beautiful, she is like a doll."

She was polite and pleasant, but for me it was like talking to a stranger, we had no emotional ties. The experience of connecting with my siblings was totally lost in our childhood.

"You have a beautiful house, Mira," I told her.

"Thank you, it was my in-laws', my husband inherited it."

Mother came in with Melie. She looked old, her hair was gray now, she didn't have any makeup on, her eyes welled up.

"Lissa! I didn't expect you."

I introduced them, "My husband Charles, my daughter Vicki, this is my mother, Angelika."

They shook hands. And she talked to Vicki, "Hi pretty girl, I'm your Grandma Angel."

"Mother, we are not staying long, we will be moving away pretty soon and I might never come back to this area, Melie said you wanted to see me... Would you like to talk now?"

"Yes, would you mind sitting outside on the deck?"

Mira served some refreshments to Charles and Vicki, and Mother and I walked alone outside.

She started, "Lissa, I have had much time lately to think about my life, our lives. I know I was not the mother you deserved, I neglected you. I was selfish and I never gave any thought to it until you came back and did what you did. First I got angry, but after a while I could not but admire your courage. That's when it all became clear to me.

When I was a little girl I looked up to my mother and saw a beautiful woman, and she was also smart, she spoke politely, I knew I was nothing like her, I always felt inferior. My mother was hard on me and she reminded me that she wanted me to be and do better, for that reason I resented her…

When you were born I was disappointed only because you looked so much like my mother. She was happy and took over you since the first day, reminding me that she was going to make someone special out of you, that you would not be a failure like I was, uneducated and married to a drunk bully. Saying that, she reminded me that I was not good enough and I became more resentful.

During the time you were growing up, I became numb to you and your needs, I didn't nurture or protect you... What I did was wrong, I extended the hostile feelings I had towards my mother to you, and now I am very remorseful.

You are my daughter, my prettiest, smartest daughter, and I am sorry, so sorry. Please forgive me, Lissa."

She was crying. I was calm and didn't have a tear to spare, I had cried so much during my childhood and younger years for what happened in my household. I felt compassion for her and understood her pain. She was weak and lost herself in her feelings of low self-esteem, she lost a lifetime…

There were no terms of endearment between us, no bond. I only pity her.

"Mother, thank you for opening up, I hope this brings you peace of mind. You just confirmed what I came to understand, that you bestowed on me the hostile feelings you had towards your mother. You are right about my Grandma, she was very influential in my life, even though I only had her for eight short years her influence propelled me into being the woman I am now. I am proud I was like her and I am sorry you never thought you were good enough to learn from your mother…

I was your child and there is nothing I can do about the choices you made. I don't know if you can truly evaluate the suffering you caused me. The harm done, the emotional scars can't be made right, can't be erased. I can't say that all is forgotten because it is not. But I want you to know that I don't harbor resentment towards you, I let it all go. I can honestly say that my heart is free. That is what I understand forgiveness is. I came here today because I didn't want to leave things unresolved.

You didn't nurture or love me, but you were the one that gave me life, and for that I am grateful."

"Lissa, you are speaking like my mother used to talk to me… You are so much like her."

"That's a compliment. I kept my Grandma's legacy of feelings and words alive in my life. Her physical death did not take her away from my heart."

She lowered her head, dried her tears, "You were more hers than mine. Please believe me when I say I am proud of you, and I wish you and your family the very best, Lissa."

"I wish you the same, Mother."

I got up, she didn't try to hug me, I didn't either.

We walked back into the house. Melie was playing with Vicki, sitting on the floor. Charles was listening to Mira talking about her family, her husband's business… She asked me, "Would you like to stay for lunch, Lissa?"

"Thank you, Mira, but we have a lot to do at home, packing, et cetera…"

Melie insisted, "Please stay a little longer, I miss you and Vicki already…"

We hugged, "We'll miss you too, Melie. Call, text and come on your vacations… I love you."

"I love you always, Lissa, always."

Mira gave me a hug, "If you come back this way, please stay with us, we can catch up."

I responded, "Thank you."

Mother stood there, "When is your baby due?"

"In January, a new baby in the new year."

She looked at me and pointed to my necklace. "My mother used to have a pearl necklace just like yours, she wore it all the time."

"I remember, Grandma told me it was going to be mine one day... This one was a gift from our Grandmother Victoria on my wedding day!"

"So did you name your daughter after your grandmother-in-law?"

"After my two grandmothers, Vicki's name is Victoria Eden."

When we got to the front door she opened her arms, "Can I hug you?"

We hugged, she whispered, "My daughter, my beautiful daughter, thank you for coming."

Just then, only then, I felt like crying, but I didn't.

"Goodbye, Mother. I wish you have a good life here with Mira."

We left.

On the way back I shed a few tears of relief.

"It was pretty emotional for you, wasn't it, Lis?"

"Emotional... And I didn't want to cry in front of her, I was not sure she was absolutely sincere in her expressions of regret."

"I understand, but I am glad we came, you can leave it all behind, we are about to cross the border..."

"Goodbye, West Virginia!"

By the end of the summer Charles listed his apartment with a realtor. We said goodbye to our friends and coworkers and decided to spend our last day in DC driving and walking around the city.

We went for a walk with our daughter in the stroller on the National Mall overlooking the Washington Monument at one end and the Capitol at the other.

I was feeling melancholic...

"We won't be seeing this view for a while... Will you miss it, Lis?"

"I'll miss DC, it will be a happy memory of the time we met, when we fell in love and started our family. It's our daughter's birthplace, we will bring her here someday."

"I'll miss it too, I lived here for so long. I met you here and I think of how we were drawn to each other since the beginning and I knew in my heart it was right. That was surprising to me, I was getting accustomed to my solitude until you came along, and I knew I wanted more, we had a solid connection, and you were the partner that I could count on to satisfy my yearnings. You completed me, Lis, I am so glad I married you and I am getting your support in this new chapter of our lives! I love you!"

"Chuck, I was complex, you enlightened me, and I found the essence of who I am, the sense of emptiness was gone…

You are my anchor and I truly believe that there is nothing that we can't overcome together, we share many commonalities and we can kindly compromise on our differences.

Above all, we love each other, and I couldn't be happier than being married to you!"

*"There could have been no two hearts so open, no tastes so similar, no feelings so in unison, no countenances so beloved."*26

That evening, on our last night in our apartment…

"Dad called, he told me that when you are ready he will introduce you to the influential people he knows in the Cedar Rapids media, he is well connected, not that you need it, but he said he'll be proud of showing you off.

He also said that he is in contact with the builder of Colin's house and he has outstanding new models. You can choose the one you like the most, and we will build the house of your dreams, darling!"

"Oh, the house of my dreams! Our house, Chuck!"

*"When I have a house of my own, I shall be miserable if I have not an excellent library."*27

"I feel nostalgic looking outside at the lights reflecting on the river down below… Tomorrow we are flying to Iowa to embark on our new life. Will everything be alright?"

"We will have an identical view like this on the Cedar River and we will arrive just in time to participate in our first Fall Festival with our family."

"Chuck, do you promise me that this is the last move? I love this city. We were rooted here, and you know how important it is for me to be settled.

I want to live in a place forever, where we can raise our children, grow a garden... I need the assurance of being permanent, enough of wandering around, feeling unsettled."

"I promise you, darling, this is it! We will travel out of Iowa only on business or to visit friends, but Splendland is and always will be our home! We will be happy there and let's see what life brings us next..."

"For starters a new baby in January! Do you think you can keep a secret from Mom until the baby is born? She is going to be so surprised to have a new granddaughter named after her, Madeline, our Madeline Marie, I love Marie, it is such a sweet and pure name, isn't it?"

"Mom will be so happy! You will have to fight her to be able to hold our baby. Mom and Grandma Tori always wanted a little girl in the house, now they will have two of them!"

"And I will have the time to write my first book, it is already outlined."

"Your book! What is it all about, darling?"

"It's based on the real life story of a Gypsy girl who went out in the world and all of her dreams came true!"

***

ACKNOWLEDGMENT

My deepest gratitude to my daughter Stephanie for her unwavering incentive and support.

***

REFERENCES

The following quotes are from Jane Austen's novels:

Page

5   *"To be fond of dancing was a certain step towards falling in love..."*1 (Pride and Prejudice)*

7   *"I declare after all there is no enjoyment like reading!"*2 (Pride and Prejudice)*

7   *"Think only of the past as its remembrance gives you pleasure."*3 (Pride and Prejudice)*

13   *"I think him everything that is worthy and amiable."*4 (Sense and Sensibility)*

27   *"It is not time or opportunity that is to determine intimacy; it is disposition alone. Seven years would be insufficient to make some people acquainted with each other, and seven days are more than enough for others."*5 (Sense and Sensibility)*

39   *"Shyness is only the effect of a sense of inferiority in some way or other. If I could persuade myself that my manners were perfectly easy and graceful, I should not be shy."*6 (Sense and Sensibility)*

40   *"She was stronger alone..."*
    "I will be calm; I will be mistress of myself."*7 (Sense and Sensibility)

40   *"Her heart did whisper that he had done it for her."*8 (Pride and Prejudice)*

44   *"[She]... told herself likewise not to hope. But it was too late. Hope had already entered..."*9 (Sense and Sensibility)*

53   *"The more I know of the world, the more am I convinced that I shall never see a man whom I can really love."*10 (Sense and Sensibility)*

56   *"But remember that the pain of parting from friends will be felt by everybody at times, whatever be their education or state."*[11] *(Sense and Sensibility)*

57   *"My idea of good company... is the company of clever, well-informed people, who have a great deal of conversation; that is what I call good company."*[12] *(Persuasion)*

64   *"I wish, as well as everybody else, to be perfectly happy; but, like everybody else, it must be in my own way."*[13] *(Sense and Sensibility)*

68   *"Where so many hours have been spent in convincing myself that I am right, is there not some reason to fear I may be wrong?"*[14] *(Sense and Sensibility)*

71   *"Angry people are not always wise..."*[15] *(Pride and Prejudice)*

83   *"She hoped to be wise and reasonable in time..."*[16] *(Persuasion)*

89   *"Pray, pray be composed... and do not betray what you feel to everybody present."*[17] *(Sense and Sensibility)*

90   *"One does not love a place the less for having suffered in it, unless it has been all suffering, nothing but suffering..."*[18] *(Persuasion)*

95   *"Till this moment I never knew myself."*[19] *(Pride and Prejudice)*

99   *"You pierce my soul. I am half agony, half hope... I have loved none but you."*[20] *(Persuasion)*

106   *"How shall I bear so much happiness!"*[21] *(Pride and Prejudice)*

114   *"I am the happiest creature in the world. Perhaps other people have said so before, but not one with such justice."*[22] *(Pride and Prejudice)*

123   *"To wish was to hope, and to hope was to expect."*[23] *(Sense and Sensibility)*

134   *"She was without any power, because she was without any desire of command over herself."*[24] *(Sense and Sensibility)*

136   *"The distance is nothing when one has a motive..."*[25] *(Pride and Prejudice)*

| 144 | *"There could have been no two hearts so open, no tastes so similar, no feelings so in unison, no countenances so beloved."*[26] *(Persuasion)* |
| 144 | *"When I have a house of my own, I shall be miserable if I have not an excellent library."*[27] *(Pride and Prejudice)* |

OTHER REFERENCES

Page 4 – 'At Last,' a ballad written in the 1940's by Gordon & Warren and made famous by Etta James' popular interpretation in the 1960's.

Pages 86-87 – The Journalist's Creed, a declaration written in 1914 by Walter Williams, the founder of the Missouri School of Journalism. The Creed is one of the clearest statements of values and standards of journalism throughout the world.

Page 124 – 'My Way,' an original French song by Jacques Revaux and English lyrics by Paul Anka. Popularized by Frank Sinatra in 1969.

ABOUT THE AUTHOR

M. Carolina Bento is a Portuguese-American citizen and resides in the Washington, DC area. She is the author of *Grandioso*, published in 2016. *Zingarese* is her second book. She continues to work on other novels.

www.ingramcontent.com/pod-product-compliance
Lightning Source LLC
Chambersburg PA
CBHW051950170626
46808CB00007B/2552